"Just a kiss? You're this upset about a kiss?"

Maggie's best friend, Emma, questioned.

"It's not just that," Maggie countered. "I don't know. He was opening up to me and then, boom, down came the shutters."

"You're in love with him," she stated.

Maggie laughed sharply. "Right," she said sarcastically.

"And he's falling in love with you, too," Emma continued.

"Now I know you're completely over the edge," she replied.

"I want you to be happy, that's all. I'm just mad I can't claim any responsibility for this. I wanted to be the one to introduce you to your future husband."

"Future husband?" Maggie cried. "If I ever did decide to get married, it sure wouldn't be to Ryan Conner!"

Emma just smiled with a self-satisfied air.

Dear Reader,

In Arlene James's *Desperately Seeking Daddy,* a harried, single working mom of three feels like Cinderella at the ball when Jack Tyler comes into her life. He wins over her kids, charms her mother and sets straight her grumpy boss. He's the FABULOUS FATHER of her kids' dreams—and the husband of hers!

Although the BUNDLE OF JOY in Amelia Varden's arms is not her natural child, she's loved the baby boy from birth. And now one man has come to claim her son—and her heart—in reader favorite Elizabeth August's *The Rancher and the Baby.*

Won't You Be My Husband? begins Linda Varner's trilogy HOME FOR THE HOLIDAYS, in which a woman ends up engaged to be married after a ten-minute reunion with a bad-boy hunk!

What's a smitten bookkeeper to do when her gorgeous boss asks her to be his bride—even for convenience? Run down the aisle!...in DeAnna Talcott's *The Bachelor and the Bassinet.*

In Pat Montana's *Storybook Bride,* tight-lipped rancher Kody Sanville's been called a half-breed his whole life and doesn't believe in storybook anything. So why can't he stop dreaming of being loved by Becca Covington?

Suzanne McMinn makes her debut with *Make Room for Mommy,* in which a single woman with motherhood and marriage on her mind falls for a single dad who isn't at all interested in saying "I do"...or so he thinks!

From classic love stories, to romantic comedies to emotional heart tuggers, Silhouette Romance offers six wonderful new novels each month by six talented authors. I hope you enjoy all six books this month—and every month.

Regards,

Melissa Senate,
Senior Editor

Please address questions and book requests to:
Silhouette Reader Service
U.S.: 3010 Walden Ave., P.O. Box 1325, Buffalo, NY 14269
Canadian: P.O. Box 609, Fort Erie, Ont. L2A 5X3

MAKE ROOM FOR MOMMY

Suzanne McMinn

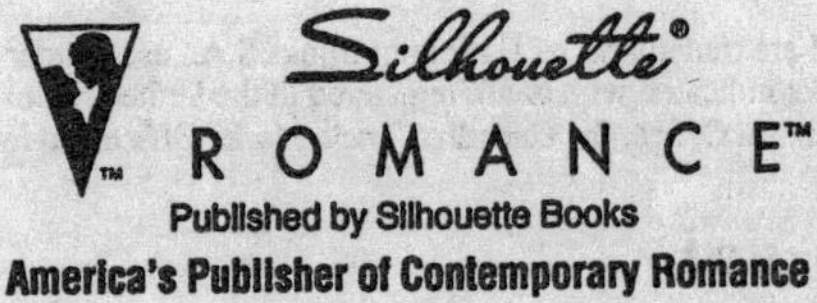

Published by Silhouette Books
America's Publisher of Contemporary Romance

For my big sister, Celeste—if it hadn't been for all those times you locked me in the kitchen pantry as a child, I probably never would have developed my imagination!

ISBN 0-373-19191-X

MAKE ROOM FOR MOMMY

This edition published by arrangement with Harlequin Books S.A.

Printed in U.S.A.

SUZANNE McMINN

lives by the lake in a small Texas town. She knew she wanted to be a writer by age five and set her sights on romance novels when she was twelve. She fulfills her dream of writing while enjoying her wonderful husband, young children and assorted dogs and cats. She loves to hear from readers and can be reached at P.O. Box 12, Granbury, TX 76048.

The Facts of Life According to Brandy Conner, Age Six

I know not everybody can have a mom. And I'm real lucky, 'cause I've got the world's best dad. But he's so grumpy sometimes—'specially when Maggie Wells comes over. She's my grown-up friend from the community center. She is *so* neat.

One of my friends says that boys act dumb sometimes when they like you. So I was thinking, what if Daddy likes Maggie? It would be so great if Maggie could live with us, like a real mom. Daddy says it's "complicated"—which means I should stop asking questions. But now *Maggie* is acting grumpy. Do you think this is a good sign?

Chapter One

"What happened to his wife?"

The social worker, Mrs. Fletcher, shifted in her cushioned swivel chair as she stared across her cluttered desk at Maggie Wells. She looked unsure of the answer she should give. The busy shuffle of activity in the community center filtered in through the open door of her cramped office.

"Does she live around here?" Maggie continued, her curiosity piqued. She watched as Mrs. Fletcher ran thick fingers through her short metallic-gray hair and sighed heavily.

"Actually," Mrs. Fletcher began in a tired tone, "we don't know that much about Mr. Conner's former wife. He's a very private person."

"Oh." Maggie thought for a moment. "But you got so much information about my background before allowing me to enter the outreach program. I guess I just assumed you knew as much about the children and their families."

The women's outreach program, organized by the Charleston community center, matched adult volunteers with young girls to provide friendship and role modeling. It was especially geared toward girls who'd lost their mothers, through death or divorce.

"I don't mean to be nosy," Maggie said hurriedly when Mrs. Fletcher didn't respond. "I just wondered. I mean, to help Brandy as much as possible, I thought it would be best if I knew something about her besides the fact that she likes dolls and roller skating."

"Yes," the social worker agreed. "I understand your interest, of course." She sat silently for a few seconds. Maggie leaned forward encouragingly and Mrs. Fletcher began to speak again. "It's simply not necessary for us to make such inquiries into personal affairs. The facts behind Mr. Conner's divorce are not our business. All we need to know is that he wishes to place his daughter in the program."

"Of course," Maggie said, straightening up in her chair, suddenly feeling as if she'd been caught trying to peep into someone's back window. "I understand entirely."

"Well, he'll be here any minute and you can meet him for yourself," Mrs. Fletcher said, breaking off and staring at the doorway of her office. Maggie turned quickly, following the social worker's gaze.

A young girl scampered eagerly into the office, a large doll clutched to her chest. But Maggie's attention was seized immediately by the dark presence that followed her, overpowering the small office with his height and brooding appearance. Her eyes moved up his torso to broad shoulders topped by a strongly angular face that held, even in January, the hint of summer's heat. Carelessly combed chestnut waves contrasted with his stern visage.

The rich luster of his hair and the smoothness of his skin, only lightly crinkled around brilliant sapphire eyes, suggested a man of no more than thirty years. But the cool glint in those blue depths intimated at a hardness inside that his age belied.

Maggie opened her mouth to greet him, but found nothing coming out.

This is so embarrassing, she thought quickly. *He'll think I'm a fool.*

Piercing blue eyes met hers for a long second, then dismissed her and passed on to Mrs. Fletcher.

Mrs. Fletcher rose and reached across her desk to extend a pudgy hand to the man who strode with an effortless assurance across the small office. Maggie, pulling herself together at last, rose also. She was graced with a cursory handshake that, despite its lack of warmth, left her hand feeling weak and crushed.

"Ryan Conner, Brandy, this is Maggie Wells," Mrs. Fletcher introduced in a businesslike monotone. Ryan Conner sat down in the chair across from Maggie, as directed by Mrs. Fletcher. His daughter perched on his knee and smiled brightly at Maggie.

"We here at the center are hoping Maggie and Brandy will be an excellent match," Mrs. Fletcher said. "You've read the materials I sent you, I assume." She looked narrowly at Ryan Conner, then went on without waiting for a response. "So you know all about Ms. Wells. She has agreed to commit to the program for at least a year, spending time with Brandy at least twice a month."

Maggie looked at Ryan, noting that he seemed impatient with the social worker's explanations. She caught his eye and smiled sympathetically, then frowned as he looked quickly away.

Mrs. Fletcher stopped, and Maggie turned her attention gladly to the child on Ryan's lap.

"Hi, Brandy," Maggie said. The six-year-old was an elflike miniature of her father in girlish form. Brown braids in the same shade as her father's hair swung against her blue woolen coat. Loose white lace tights wrinkled about her ankles as she kicked her feet against the legs of the chair.

"Hi," Brandy returned. She fidgeted on her father's knee. He put a restraining arm around her, but she pushed him back and jumped down instead. She walked over to Maggie and reached a hesitant finger out to touch an auburn curl that nestled softly against Maggie's shoulder.

"You have red hair!" she said, and giggled. Maggie laughed with her, enchanted with the little girl's honest spontaneity.

She glanced at the child's father and found him watching with a disapproving frown.

"Don't be rude, Brandy," he scolded, his voice softly Southern yet still commanding. Brandy backed away from Maggie, grinning mischievously.

"Oh, that's okay. But I do prefer to call it auburn," Maggie said to Brandy, ignoring Ryan Conner's cool expression.

But she couldn't resist looking at him again a moment later and smiling. His face remained impassive.

Really, Maggie thought, *what is his problem? We've just met! He can't dislike me already.*

"Mr. Conner—" she began.

"Ryan," he corrected. "Only my students call me Mr. Conner."

"Okay, if you'll call me Maggie," she agreed cheerfully. "You're a teacher?" she prompted, smiling at him encouragingly.

"High school English," he responded briefly.

Maggie raised an expectant brow, hoping he would elaborate yet knowing somehow that he wouldn't.

The ice has to break soon, she told herself, *or this match will never work.*

It was almost as if he had placed a wall between them before they had even met, she suddenly thought. She eyed him stubbornly.

"I'm very happy to meet you and your daughter, Mr.—Ryan, I mean," she said.

"Yes," he replied.

Yes, what? Maggie wondered, her silly streak rising to the challenge of the conversation. *Yes, it's nice for anyone to get to meet you? Yes, it's nice to meet me, too? No, no,* she decided, *he doesn't think it's nice to meet me. He looks like he wants to throw me off a cliff. Forget that I'm offering to do him a favor.*

She turned away from his uneasy survey and looked to Mrs. Fletcher for help in the silence that lay heavy in its suddenness.

The social worker took a satisfied breath and rose.

"Well," Mrs. Fletcher said, "now that everybody's introduced themselves, I'll give you a few moments to get acquainted."

She lumbered out from behind her desk and disappeared into the outer office.

Maggie felt sure she didn't breathe for at least thirty seconds. She looked across at Ryan Conner and smiled with soldierly resolve, her inner tirade forgotten in her panic at the social worker's unexpected departure. He stared back at her, head cocked slightly to the side, as if waiting for her to make the first move.

She took the easy way out and turned to Brandy.

"Brandy," Maggie began uncomfortably, "tell me about your doll. She's beautiful."

Brandy proudly held the life-size doll straight out in front of herself to show Maggie.

"Her name is Penny," Brandy said. "And she's my favorite doll, isn't she, Daddy?" She glanced up at her father and he nodded almost imperceptibly. Maggie noticed how the firm lines of his face softened slightly as he looked at his daughter.

Brandy turned the doll back toward herself and tugged Penny's rumpled red dress down. When she was satisfied, she flipped the doll back around for Maggie's further admiration.

"She's very pretty," Maggie said, showing the proper appreciation for Brandy's prize doll. "I had a doll a lot like her when I was about your age," she added, surprising herself by voicing the sudden childhood memory. The happy memory, before her father's bankruptcy, before...

Maggie blinked quickly, pushing back the painful memories that rushed in on her at the thought of her father. She was annoyed with herself for allowing the hurtful past to intrude. She took a quick, determined breath.

"Who gave Penny to you?" Maggie asked with false brightness, back in control, with the hurt neatly tucked away in long-practiced fashion.

Ryan Conner moved slightly in his chair as Brandy answered, "Mommy gave her to me. Do you still have your doll? What's her name?" Brandy asked, impatient and clearly not to be sidetracked from her own line of thought.

Maggie noticed Ryan's discomfiture, and was torn between curiosity and relief that Brandy didn't elaborate on her mother.

"Her name is Sarah," Maggie told her, carefully guarding herself from thinking beyond the doll itself. "I still have her. She's getting rather old now."

"Do you still play with her?" Brandy asked, her blue eyes bright.

Maggie grinned. "I haven't played with Sarah in a long time. I used to like to have tea parties with her, though. Do you ever have tea parties with Penny?"

Brandy nodded eagerly. "Daddy plays with me," she said.

Maggie looked directly at Ryan for the first time since Mrs. Fletcher had left the room. She tried to imagine him playing tea party with his little daughter and her doll, but couldn't quite manage it.

"If you'd like, and if it's all right with your father—" Maggie glanced at Ryan. His impenetrable azure gaze answered nothing. And asked...? She wasn't sure what. "Maybe when it warms up we can have a little tea party together, for Penny and Sarah. And Romeo, of course. He likes tea."

"Who's Romeo?" Brandy asked, moving a little farther from her father, a little closer to Maggie.

"Romeo's my cat. He's a big, fat, white cat. He just has one little patch of orange between his eyes."

"And he drinks tea?" Brandy squealed. She turned to her father and laughed, clapping her hand over her mouth in childlike glee. "Isn't that funny, Daddy?"

Ryan nodded, his lips curving slightly upward in response to his daughter's exuberance. He stretched out one long arm and, with a broad, strong hand, ruffled her dark head, so like his own, and pulled her back toward him.

Maggie's breath caught in her throat as she watched him smile.

Ryan Conner looked...human! The smile was gentle and loving, softening the squareness of his jaw into something no longer intimidating. Into something downright appealing.

Something that started a funny little tremble in her stomach. Not nerves.

Attraction.

Maggie swallowed hard, pushing back the thought, stifling the feeling. It was truly insane, and had to be squelched immediately.

Ryan lifted his gaze to Maggie then, and for a second—a heart-touching pitter-patter in time—she spied warmth and softness and...pain? Then, without warning, the mask of coolness shifted back into place.

"I want you to go find Mrs. Fletcher and tell her we're through here, Brandy," he instructed his daughter softly, his eyes turning down to meet hers. She wrinkled her nose up at him obstinately, but he set his mouth firmly and she hurried off obediently to the door, still hanging on tightly to Penny.

Maggie recrossed her legs and looked at Ryan. Having glimpsed a gentler side of the man, she felt even more uncomfortable. He'd be easier to deal with if she could decide he was an all-around jerk.

"You have a very bright daughter," she commented, trying to fill the void left by Brandy's exit.

Ryan stared narrowly at Maggie, ignoring her compliment.

"Why do you want to spend your spare time with a six-year-old girl whom you don't know and who isn't even related to you?" he asked brusquely.

Maggie's mouth dropped open in surprise at his blunt question.

"Well, you know from the information Mrs. Fletcher gave you that I'm single. I don't have any children of my own," Maggie explained. *So much for his soft side,* she thought dryly.

"I don't want to know what's on the form," Ryan cut in. "I want to know why you think you want to become a part of my daughter's life."

Maggie noticed the lightly sarcastic emphasis he placed on the word *think,* as if he didn't believe she was really serious about it.

"As Mrs. Fletcher said, I've agreed to the specifications on time that I'm willing to commit to the program," Maggie said coolly, struggling not to squirm under his unflinching gaze.

"Look," she continued, "I'm not really sure what you're trying to get at. You seem to have a problem with me."

There. It was out in the open.

He seemed unfazed.

Maggie shook her head.

"Well, it's up to you and Brandy whether I'll be assigned to work with her or not," she said. "I don't know what you want to hear, but the bottom line is just that I feel I have something to give and no one to give it to. I don't think I can be more frank than that."

"You work at a computer company, I believe," Ryan stated, completely ignoring Maggie's honest admissions.

"Yes," Maggie answered, feeling herself shrink under his tight scrutiny. She was a little rattled by his rapid change of topic. "I'm the assistant director of the local sales division." She felt better as she told him that, pride in her accomplishments shoring up her flagging confidence.

"I'm sure your job is very important to you."

"Yes, of course," Maggie agreed. "But I have plenty of time to give to Brandy, as well. I'm fully prepared to keep my commitment to her, as I've said."

Several times already, she added silently.

"I see," Ryan said quietly. "Perhaps I need to tell you why I entered Brandy in this program."

"That would be helpful, yes," Maggie agreed politely, forcing a smile to her lips. Brandy was such an appealing child. She would be a joy to work with. Getting through this strange conversation with her father would be worth it, Maggie reminded herself.

"Brandy's mother is very busy with her career," Ryan said. "She doesn't live here in Charleston. In fact, she doesn't even live in South Carolina. She's in Atlanta," he explained, his face expressionless. "I entered Brandy in the women's outreach program because she hardly ever sees her mother. But I don't want her put in the same position with you that she's in with her mother."

"I don't think that would be a problem, as I've already tried to explain," Maggie broke in. "I think Brandy and I could get along quite well, and I promise I'll be there for her."

Ryan appeared thoughtful, then fixed his gaze on Maggie in an assessing manner.

"I wonder whether you work a great deal of overtime," he suggested. "I don't want someone who'll be canceling out on Brandy every time a crisis comes up at the office. She already has that."

Maggie stared back at Ryan, carefully holding her gaze steady.

"I've already assured you that won't happen," she said sharply. She sighed and rose. Then, with an ease that came from years of practice pretending an assurance that she didn't always feel, she flipped back the curls that fell forward across her shoulders.

She wondered if that glimpse of softness she'd witnessed a few moments earlier had existed only in her imagination.

"I'm sorry, Mr. Conner. I see that I'm just not what you're looking for," Maggie continued, enunciating each word with a cool precision that she hoped hid the nervous roiling of her stomach. "I think you decided that before you got here today." As she reached the door, she couldn't resist looking back and adding a challenge. "Too bad. You'll never know now, will you?"

Turning away, she almost bumped into Brandy and Mrs. Fletcher. She said goodbye without stopping and escaped the community center quickly. Reaching the parking lot, she inhaled the sweet, fresh odor of South Carolina winter pine and tried to stanch the rushing tide of pent-up nerves.

"I made such a fool of myself, Emma," Maggie moaned. She buried her face in her hands and leaned back into the couch in the living room of her suburban Charleston home. "I handled it all wrong. The man detested me. That was obvious from the start. And there I was, practically begging him to let me help him with his daughter. It was ridiculous."

"Oh, Mag, it couldn't have been that bad, could it?" Emma Mathison asked, laughing. "You make this man sound like an ogre."

Maggie lifted her head and stared at Emma, brows raised.

"Okay, he does sound a bit primitive," Emma conceded, hazel eyes twinkling in a narrow face framed by short, dark, salon-created waves. "I'll give you that. But didn't you say he was good-looking?"

Maggie had to smile at that. Emma had been trying to set her up with a man and marry her off since their third year of college when Emma quit school and married a dentist. A house, a dog and two small children later, Emma never let an opportunity slip to try to bring Maggie into the ranks of wedded women.

"Don't even start, Em," Maggie said. "Believe me, this man is not a possibility. For starters, he hates me. And even if he didn't, I definitely don't like him. I'm not even attracted to him." That was a lie, but it felt good to say it. "And when did I say he was good-looking, anyway?"

Strong, firm features and mysterious eyes flashed into her mind. She tried to push the image away, but the vague impression of hurt in his blue depths stayed with her.

"Okay," she admitted, determined to ignore the troubling sensations her thoughts evoked. She smiled at Emma playfully. "So he was handsome." Maggie leaned back. "But, so what? I'm telling you, I'm not interested."

"What else is new?" Emma teased in the same familiar tone she always used when Maggie turned aside her attempts to interest her in romance.

"None of this matters, anyway," Maggie reminded her. "He was so rude. I just don't understand it. He doesn't even know me, and he seemed to be assigning all these rotten characteristics to me."

Emma drank the last of her coffee and set the cup down on a coaster on the end table. Rising, she said, "Well, I've got to go pick up the boys from my mom's. Don't brood, Maggie," she warned, shaking one well-manicured finger Maggie's way. "It'll make you wrinkle."

Maggie followed her friend to the door. Shutting it after Emma, she wandered thoughtfully into the kitchen, picking a tub of low-calorie fruit yogurt out of the refrigerator. Then she returned to the functional blue couch in the living room and plopped down again. The package made a soft pop as she tore off the aluminum cover. A large white cat jumped up beside her and mewed.

"Oh, Romeo," Maggie whispered to the cat. "Forget it. I'm not sharing my yogurt." She ruffled the long fur between his ears and pushed him down from the couch.

I can't believe how everything turned out, she thought, her mind turning back to her meeting with Ryan Conner.

She remembered her excitement a month earlier when she'd seen the article in the newspaper about the community center. The section detailing the women's outreach program had caught her eye as she'd been picking at a TV dinner late one night after work. As she read the story describing the community center's program, she was inspired to volunteer. She had Emma—her best friend—and her neighbors and co-workers, but something was missing. She hadn't known just what until she'd read that article.

Maggie felt an empathy born of experience for children growing up with only one parent. She wanted to share her life with a child, to share the innocence and joy that had been cut short in her own childhood.

Through satisfying a child's need in this way she hoped to fill the void—past and future—in her own life. At twenty-eight, she'd begun to think it was a very real possibility that she would never marry and have a child of her own.

Now it looked as if her chances of taking part in the life of sweet, bright Brandy Conner were pretty dim, too. And all because of the child's insufferable father, Maggie thought with irritation.

She swallowed a spoonful of strawberry-banana yogurt. Who was she kidding? she berated herself. She certainly hadn't done her cause any good by walking out on him. If she could have just gotten past the first meeting, she was sure she wouldn't have had to have much to do with him after she was paired up with Brandy. After all, she was supposed to befriend the child, not the father.

And what was all that stuff about his wife? she wondered. He obviously had some ridiculous problem with self-sufficient women. He didn't seem to understand that some women wanted—or needed—to work.

Maggie knew about need, about desperation. The picture of her own mother dragging home late at night after hours of cleaning offices or waiting tables intruded into her thoughts. Later, Maggie, too, learned to wait tables, but only long enough to work her way through college and earn her business degree.

But working and studying had left little time for a social life, and despite Emma's dubious help, Maggie had rarely dated during college. The dates were even fewer and farther between after she began her career. Her job made up for it, she always told herself. Her work made her feel good, and she was good at it. She depended on herself, and no one else.

And Ryan Conner could go jump in a lake if he thought he had a right to criticize her for it, she thought defensively.

Maggie sat up and put the barely touched carton of yogurt down on the coffee table, leaving the cat to stretch up and sniff at it unhindered. Maggie rose and walked down the hall to her bedroom at the back of the house.

In contrast to the modern functional decor of the living room, Maggie's bedroom, her private retreat, was traditional and romantic. A four-poster bed dominated the spacious and utterly feminine room decorated with white lace curtains and a white comforter. Maggie lay down across the cool white spread and tried to clear her mind of Ryan and the disappointing episode at the community center. She tried to force herself to concentrate on work, on the next week's projects.

She closed her eyes and saw Ryan Conner's soft smile.

"Daddy?"

Ryan hesitated, his fingers curved over the switch to his daughter's bedside lamp. The book he had read aloud a chapter from—as per their usual evening ritual—lay closed on his lap. Brandy often fell asleep before he finished reading an entire chapter. Tonight she was awake. Wide-awake.

There was something about the way she spoke that caught his attention and made him freeze. She was worried about something.

"What is it, sweetie?" Ryan asked. Softly his fingers swept along her small, rounded cheekbone.

"Why don't you like Maggie?" Brandy asked, her voice low in the stillness of her bedroom.

Snapping emerald eyes and rich auburn hair flashed into Ryan's thoughts. And that scent that had surrounded her, like peaches ripe in a summer-hot grove, tempting and sweet.

He knew the answer to Brandy's question. He knew exactly why he didn't like Maggie Wells. He was afraid she might turn out to be too much like Delia, Brandy's mother—who always seemed to have plenty of good intentions, but never the time to carry them out.

He'd approached the community center program with cautious optimism from the start. He knew Brandy could benefit enormously from the opportunity—but he wanted to be very certain that he didn't set his little daughter up for a disappointing experience.

Still, in spite of all his concerns, he'd been attracted to Maggie at an immediate, undeniable, gut level. So attracted, that the careful wall he'd formed after his divorce had very nearly crumbled during their meeting.

"What gave you the idea that I didn't like her?" Ryan asked, sidetracking to another question.

Brandy's blue eyes stared back unwaveringly.

"I don't know," she answered simply. "I just didn't think you did."

Ryan laughed and ruffled his daughter's hair with a careless brush of his hand. He leaned forward and kissed her cheek.

"I'm sure she's a very nice lady," Ryan told her. "You know what? I bet you're going to get to meet lots of nice ladies at the community center, and you'll get to choose one to be your very own special friend."

"I want Maggie to be my special friend." Brandy reached out and took her father's hand. "Please."

Ryan looked down at the small hand in his, then back up to the pleading expression in Brandy's eyes. And he remembered the flash in Maggie's gaze when he'd demanded to know why she wanted to be part of his daughter's life.

She felt she had something to give, she'd said, and no one to give it to. She had no husband, no child of her own.

He couldn't help but wonder why. Had she made work her whole life?

The spark in Maggie's eyes when she'd talked about her job hadn't passed Ryan by. He'd seen that kind of spark before. At the time, it had been walking out the door, leaving him to raise Brandy alone.

"Doesn't Maggie want to be my friend?" Brandy asked. A crack broke through her voice on the last word.

"Oh, sweetheart." Ryan leaned down and hugged his daughter. "I didn't mean that. I just meant that you don't have to make a decision right away. Mrs. Fletcher is going to introduce you to some other nice ladies, too."

"But I don't want anybody else," Brandy persisted. "I want Maggie."

"Why?" Ryan asked, genuinely surprised by Brandy's insistence on Maggie Wells. After all, they'd spent only five minutes together. Ryan had hoped Brandy would forget all about her.

But apparently his daughter was having as much trouble clearing her mind of Maggie as he was. He'd been haunted all day by her heart-shaped face and luscious fall of red curls, and pained by the old memories she stirred inside him.

"I like Maggie," Brandy said softly. She chewed her bottom lip. "Doesn't she like me?"

"Of course she likes you, sweetie," Ryan assured her.

"Will you call Mrs. Fletcher and tell her I want Maggie?"

Ryan hesitated. Seconds passed in silence.

Too bad, Maggie had said to him coolly as she'd left the community center. *You'll never know,* she'd added.

Never know what?

"Please, Daddy."

Chapter Two

Water dripped from Maggie as she hurried from the bathroom to the shrilling brass phone in her bedroom. Damp footprints marked her path across the plush tan rug. She grabbed the receiver as she fumbled to wrap a towel around her wet form.

"Miss Wells?" the familiar gravelly voice inquired.

"Yes. This is Mrs. Fletcher, isn't it?" Maggie asked. She experienced the little sinking feeling that always came to her when she knew someone was going to give her bad news.

"I've spoken with Mr. Conner," Mrs. Fletcher said. "He says Brandy wants you. He'd like to go ahead and sign you up with her. Do you accept?"

Maggie gasped. Had that horrible conversation with Ryan Conner really taken place last week, or was that just a nightmare? What could have changed his mind? For a few seconds she considered whether she should say no. Or tell Mrs. Fletcher she'd have to think about it. After all, how could she work with this man's child? What if he kept acting the same way toward her?

Oh, who cares about him? she decided in a flash. *Brandy is the one who matters.*

"Yes," she agreed quickly before she could change her mind.

"Fine," Mrs. Fletcher said. "Now, it's going to be up to you to set up the days and times to see Brandy. Remember to clear all your plans with her father first. Let me give you his phone number and address. Be sure to tell me when your first outing is scheduled so I can check back with you to see how things are going."

Maggie grabbed a pad and pen from her night table and shakily wrote down Ryan's phone number and address. After saying goodbye to Mrs. Fletcher, she set the phone down and sank onto the bed, heedless of the spreading wet splotch she made as she soaked into the downy white comforter. She stared at the ceiling.

Should she call him now?

She sat up. Yes, she answered herself, she should do it now, before she lost her nerve. She stared numbly at the piece of notepaper that held Ryan Conner's phone number. She picked it up, then set it back down as if the paper had burned her fingers.

She stared at the notepaper again. She could see Ryan Conner's clear, cold stare in her memory. Then she remembered Brandy's earnest blue eyes, gazing hopefully at her.

Maggie picked up her pen and quickly punched in Ryan's phone number.

"Hello."

Maggie swallowed tightly.

"Mr. Conner—I mean, Ryan, this is Maggie Wells."

Good start, she chided herself.

"Yes?"

Maggie fingered the edge of her thick, damp towel.

"I'm calling about seeing Brandy next weekend, if that's all right," she said. "Mrs. Fletcher called me today."

"What time do you want to see her?" Ryan asked. His voice was businesslike and polite, without the animosity he had formerly shown, yet still lacking warmth.

"Well, there's a miniatures exhibit at the civic center this Saturday. I thought Brandy might like to see it," Maggie suggested, gaining confidence. "It starts at ten o'clock."

"Fine."

"Can I talk to—" Maggie began, but stopped short as she realized he had already hung up. She shook her head in frustration.

She put down the receiver and lay back on her soft bed, staring up at the ceiling. She hoped she hadn't just made a terrible mistake.

Maggie pressed slowly on the brake, easing her car to a smooth halt in front of Ryan Conner's house. The long, one-story gray brick house sat back from the road, partially hidden from the street by a stand of pine trees. The house occupied a large lot in a rural area just outside Charleston. From the large bare patch at the side of the house, Maggie could see Ryan was a gardener. This surprised her, and then she wondered why it should.

After all, she didn't really know anything about him. And based on his previous behavior, she had no reason to think that was going to change, she reminded herself.

He'll probably just push Brandy out the door without a word, she thought dryly.

Maggie took a deep breath and stepped out, slamming the door of her shiny silver sports car behind her. Her low heels clicked loudly in the quiet country air as she followed the flagged walkway to the front door. Grabbing the brass knocker, she banged loudly.

The door opened so quickly, she knew someone must have been watching her approach. The knocker fairly flew from Maggie's hand as Brandy yanked the door wide, a broad smile lighting her small face.

"Hi, Maggie!" she cried. "I'm almost ready. I just need my jacket."

Brandy tore off into the inner reaches of the house, leaving Maggie standing on the doorstep. Ryan Conner stepped forward toward the door.

"Maggie," he said, sounding oddly uncomfortable with her name. "Come in. Please."

Maggie forced a smile to her lips.

He's being polite, she thought. *Be polite back.*

"Thank you," she said carefully, and followed his outstretched arm. She was surprised to find how large the house looked once she was inside. The living room was light and spacious with wide windows giving view to a wooded backyard that seemed greatly devoted to Brandy's play. An elaborate swing set dominated a wide-open space between some pines, while a rudimentary tree house sat low in an oak.

"This is a lovely home," Maggie commented.

Ryan didn't ask her to sit down, so she stood and looked about with interest, determined not to let him bother her. She would be out of there in just a few minutes, she reminded herself, with the whole day to spend with Brandy alone.

She tried to concentrate on the view, but her eyes were drawn back to the man standing quietly at her side.

How tall he was. Maggie's slim height came close to that of many men, an asset in the business world, she'd always thought. But as she stood in the living room beside Ryan, she realized he was at least four inches taller than she was.

Ryan started to gesture Maggie to the couch, then stopped himself. He hesitated to take that extra step toward friendliness, afraid in his heart of where it might lead.

Maggie was supposed to be Brandy's friend, not his. And while easing the tension between them might seem to pave the way to a smoother relationship for Brandy and Maggie, Ryan knew that it could set a dangerous precedent.

As much as he feared Maggie might turn out to be like Delia, she appealed to him on an even deeper, more sensual, level. Maintaining the tension preserved the distance.

Ryan turned his back on Maggie and stared out the window at the dry winter day. Hands stuffed in his jeans pockets, he willed his daughter to hurry back with her jacket.

Brandy arrived suddenly in the living room, breathless from a run down the hallway, pulling on her jacket as she came. Ryan swiveled back around at the sound of her approach, grateful to no longer be alone with Maggie.

"I'm ready," Brandy announced with youthful exuberance for the anticipated treat.

"Great," Maggie said, grinning at her enthusiasm. Turning to Ryan, she added, "As I told you on the phone, we'll be going to the civic center to see the miniatures show.

"There will be all kinds of dolls and dollhouses on display," she continued, looking at Brandy. The little girl's eyes lit up.

"Should I bring Penny?" Brandy asked.

Maggie laughed. "Oh, I don't think so. What if you lost her among all the dolls at the show? I think you'd better leave her here," she advised.

"Okay," Brandy agreed, placing her hand in Maggie's. "Let's go."

Maggie looked down at the small hand in her own, touched by Brandy's warmth and easy acceptance. As they reached the door, Maggie turned back to say goodbye to Ryan and tell him when to expect them back. She was surprised to see him donning a brown suede jacket.

"You're going out?" she asked.

"Yes," he said, looking at her strangely. "I'm going with you."

"You're going with us?" Maggie repeated, her heart skipping a beat. "Why?"

"Do you have a problem with that?" he asked, as if she, rather than he, were the one suggesting something out of place.

"Well, I guess . . . I mean, I don't think that's the idea, do you?" she asked, fumbling to express herself and realizing she was not doing a very good job of it.

"Have you got a set of rules?" he challenged. Her expression of disbelief amused him as well as intrigued him. Apparently she wasn't any more eager to spend time with him than he was to spend time with her. But in this case, he was determined to insist. He had to make sure that allowing Maggie Wells into Brandy's life had been the correct choice. He couldn't simply let a complete stranger take his six-year-old daughter on an outing.

And since Brandy would be with them on this expedition, there would no worry of his dealing with Maggie alone. He wouldn't have any trouble maintaining the distance between them.

Maggie stiffened as she stared at Brandy's father. She could hardly believe what she was hearing from Ryan Conner. He acted as if he didn't trust her to care for Brandy alone!

Okay, Maggie, take a deep one, she told herself.

She breathed deep and smiled. It felt a little unnatural on her lips, but she was sure it looked all right.

"Well, then, let's go, shall we?" she suggested amicably, taking Brandy along with her out the door. Fighting Ryan on this when they were about to walk out the door would do no good, Maggie decided. Acquiesce, and live to battle another day.

She heard Ryan pulling the door shut as he followed them down the flagstone walk. Maggie hurried down the long path toward the street to her car until Brandy suddenly tugged on her arm. Maggie looked at Brandy, and followed her gaze back toward the house where Ryan stood in the driveway unlocking the door to a dark blue four-door sedan.

Ryan looked up and met her gaze coolly.

Maggie released a sigh and, slipping her car keys into her purse, walked with Brandy to the blue sedan. Brandy jumped in the back, leaving the front to Ryan and Maggie.

Ryan backed out of the driveway wordlessly while Brandy chattered away, leaning forward between the front seats as far as her seat belt would let her to talk to her father and Maggie. Aside from warning Brandy several times to sit back, Ryan listened quietly for the most part, allowing Maggie to talk to his daughter.

Glancing at Ryan from the corner of her eye, Maggie observed how his face softened whenever he spoke to Brandy.

He really adores her, Maggie thought. He appeared a completely different person with his daughter.

What do I do to make him react so harshly? Maggie wondered. He was clearly capable of gentleness.

I'm not even asking for gentleness, she thought, smiling to herself. Mere civility would do.

Her eyes met his and she didn't try to hide her smile.

His brows furrowed in response, and he stared hard at the road.

Ryan found himself oddly irritated by Maggie's seemingly unfaltering cheer. He felt anything but cheerful himself, caught as he was between desire and apprehension.

It was going to take a lot more than her word—or her smile—to convince Ryan that Maggie's dedication to Brandy was genuine and lasting. The women's outreach program might have sounded appealing to her on the face of it, but taking on the responsibility of being part of a child's life could involve sacrifices and commitments that Maggie Wells wasn't expecting.

Not everyone was willing to make those sacrifices and commitments. Especially for someone else's child. More than one promising relationship had ended for Ryan after the women learned he had sole custody of a young child. The experiences had made him all the more protective of Brandy—and of himself. Neither one of them needed any more disappointments.

Maggie chatted with Brandy about the various things they might see at the show as Ryan continued to drive silently. Relief swept over her when they arrived downtown at last. The three of them filed in behind a crowd of exhibitgoers.

We look just like a typical little family, Maggie thought, the notion coming to her from out of the blue. *These people probably look at us and think we're married.*

Now why did she think of that? She shook herself mentally and turned to Brandy, determined to focus on the little girl.

Brandy and Maggie wandered through the large open hall for several hours, stopping at every display table. Brandy peered and gasped with wonder at the intricate miniatures and the fancy dolls. Maggie enjoyed the light in Brandy's eyes every time the little girl saw something that particularly excited her. Ryan followed along behind them slowly, staying just far enough back to make it almost seem as if he weren't there.

"Look!" Brandy cried. "They're real little playing cards! They have numbers and pictures and everything."

Brandy leaned comfortably on Maggie and pressed her nose against the glass display case. Maggie turned around to find Ryan staring at her, his forehead knitted in thought.

She tried smiling at him, but he looked away.

Finally Brandy had seen everything except the children's puppet show that played every half hour. Maggie settled her on the floor near the puppet stage and retreated to the back of the theater area where Ryan waited, arms crossed, a bored expression on his face.

Maggie stood beside him and stared at the puppet show with unseeing eyes, trying to ignore the fact that he was ignoring her. Five minutes later, she knew it was no use. She couldn't stand it. She turned and faced his stern profile.

"Mr. Conner."

He looked at her blandly.

At least he knows I'm alive, she thought.

"Ryan." The word came out of his mouth in a short clip.

"Of course," Maggie said. *He does hate it when I call him Mr. Conner,* she thought. Her lips curved upward slightly. "Sorry," she said.

He turned away again.

"Wait a minute," Maggie said. He looked back at her. "I think we should talk. I don't know why you came here with us today, or what exactly your problem is with me. I just know that you agreed to allow me to work with Brandy. Obviously you decided I could provide something your daughter needs. You might as well let me do it."

The words had tumbled out before she could think them through, but she knew they had to be said. Things couldn't go on this way.

"Why do you disapprove of me?" she demanded when he didn't respond to her outburst.

"Disapprove?" he repeated so softly, she could barely hear him over the laughter of the children.

"I don't know. Disapprove, or whatever." Maggie shook her head. "Look, you're the one who told Mrs. Fletcher you wanted me to work with Brandy."

"Brandy chose you, not I," he corrected. "I want what's best for Brandy. She doesn't always know what's best for herself. Sometimes I let her make her own decisions, but I don't want to see her get hurt. I want to make sure that allowing her to make this decision was right."

"You have to give me a chance if you're ever going to find that out," Maggie retorted hotly. "You don't need to tag along with us or drive us around in your car."

He cocked his head and, for the first time, Maggie thought she detected the glimmer of a grin on his face.

"I don't find this amusing," she said, surprising herself at the rising anger she felt. "I'm not playing games here."

"Oh, no?" he questioned, all evidence of the grin gone. "You want to play at having a part-time daughter who you can put away and take out whenever you want to."

"That's ridiculous," Maggie answered quickly.

"Really?" he asked. "Why aren't you married, with a family of your own?"

Maggie was speechless for a moment. Who did Ryan Conner think he was, questioning her about her marital status? Her stomach tightened as she stifled the indignant question.

For Brandy's sake, she'd stop before the conversation degenerated into a shouting match.

"You know, I think I'll just wait in one of those chairs by the wall," she said coldly, abruptly leaving Ryan.

Maggie was still fuming when Brandy rushed over, flushed with laughter, dragging her father behind her.

It's going to be a long ride home, Maggie thought.

To Maggie's relief, it was weeks later before she shared the same air space with Ryan in an automobile again. This time it was in her own car.

And she gained a perverse pleasure from the entire episode.

Ryan had not joined Maggie and Brandy on an outing since that first time until Brandy had requested that her two favorite "big people" go to the movies together with her.

Maggie firmly suggested they go in her car and restrained her laughter when Ryan acquiesced to Brandy's request that she be allowed to sit up front with Maggie. He couldn't have realized how small her back seat was when he'd agreed to his daughter's plan, and Maggie felt no compunction to warn him. He hadn't complained about the inconvenience, however, as he sat, knees hunched, in the back seat of Maggie's sports car.

Throughout the afternoon he remained his usual quiet self. The nearly two months since he had met Maggie had made him no less distant than he'd been that day in Mrs. Fletcher's office. With that confrontation in the exhibit hall still replaying itself in Maggie's mind, she hadn't been eager to instigate conversation herself. Fortunately, moviegoing naturally necessitated little talk. And Brandy took care of filling what otherwise might have been silence in the car.

"Can we stop and look at the alligators, Daddy? Please!" Brandy begged on their way home from the movie theater, turning to her father with pleading eyes.

Maggie glanced back and witnessed the harsh planes of Ryan's face softening as he smiled at his daughter. She knew now that it hadn't been her imagination that Ryan Conner had a soft side.

She just couldn't figure out why his daughter was the only one who got the benefit of it.

Ryan nodded his agreement to Brandy's plan, and Maggie pulled her car over onto the dirt just past the narrow two-lane bridge that spanned a swamp. Brandy had shown her the spot and talked her into stopping to look for 'gators several times already since they'd first met.

As the car rolled to a halt, Brandy jumped out, ran to the guardrail at the side of the low bridge and peered over. Maggie held back a smile as Ryan uncurled his muscular length from the back seat. He rose to his full height, then bent to rub the back of one knee. He straightened and looked up, meeting Maggie's amused gaze.

Serves you right, she thought.

"I hope you weren't too uncomfortable back there," she said aloud in a sweetly solicitous voice.

"Not at all," Ryan replied evenly. Eyeing his daughter, he called out, "Be careful, Brandy. Don't lean over too far."

Ryan had spied the twinkle in Maggie's green eyes that told him she found it highly entertaining that he'd endured a ride in the back seat of her sports car. He knew he should by all rights be irritated with her. But he wasn't.

Instead, he'd spent the afternoon absorbing how wonderful she was with his daughter, what a genuine rapport they'd clearly developed. In the weeks since she'd been matched with Brandy, Maggie had kept to her word about meeting with Brandy every two weeks, and had determinedly sought out activities that the little girl enjoyed.

The bottom line was that Brandy had never seemed happier. Ryan was forced to give the credit for that to Maggie.

Waiting by the car, Ryan watched Brandy. Not immediately spying any alligators, the little girl grabbed Maggie's arm and pulled her across the empty road to try the other side. Ryan followed and stood quietly beside Maggie as Brandy ran up and down the guardrail searching for signs of reptilian life below.

Maggie smiled as she glanced at Ryan standing beside her. The warm early March breeze, carrying a hint of the ocean's salty scent across the inland swamp, softly ruffled his dark hair. *He* is *handsome,* Maggie thought as she watched him, remembering her first conversation with Emma about Ryan. She noted how relaxed Ryan's face appeared, not stern and tense the way she usually saw him.

She found herself noticing little things, such as how long his eyelashes were for a man. Then she observed the tiny laugh crinkles around his eyes that suggested a man of better humor than he had so far displayed to her. He was not as cold as he seemed, Maggie thought. She almost felt guilty for laughing to herself about his being scrunched up in the back seat.

Ryan turned and looked at her. She realized that she was staring—and that she had been caught.

"I'm sorry," Maggie said with a shaky laugh. "I was just thinking."

"About what?" Ryan asked, his eyes strangely gentle as he looked into hers.

Maggie retreated from his uncharacteristic friendliness by transferring her gaze to the murky green water below.

"I love the way the swamp looks different every time I drive by it on the way out to your house," she said, dissembling. She looked back at Ryan. "It's always changing, with each breeze. See, it's moving even now." Maggie pointed to a huge lily pad bordered by tall fur-topped cattails that shifted with the spring wind.

"Yes," Ryan agreed. "That's what I like about it, too." Then, so softly Maggie had to lean toward him slightly to hear it, he added, "It's very peaceful and uncomplicated."

For just a few seconds, she saw the familiar expression that he seemed to normally reserve only for his daughter.

You'd almost think he wanted to be friends, she pondered. *Or at least to start over as something other than enemies.*

"How's school?" Maggie asked suddenly, afraid to let the moment of fragile rapport slip away. She had never heard him talk about his work, but she often chanced upon him grading papers or buried in books when she dropped by on the weekends to pick up Brandy.

"Good," he replied in a noncommittal tone, then, surprisingly, he smiled. A smile that lit his face and sparked an odd tingle in the pit of Maggie's stomach. "It's always a challenge trying to make kids like reading the classics," he continued. "And it allows me to have school holidays and summers to spend with Brandy."

"I can see that means a lot to you," Maggie observed warmly. "It sounds like you really enjoy the work, too. I loved literature in high school myself. I still remember my twelfth-grade English teacher. I admired her so much that for a while I wanted to be an English teacher, too. I even went so far as to minor in English at college," she told him.

Ryan froze inside, suddenly wary. He recalled how he and Delia had studied English together during their college years. He'd entered the teaching profession, and Delia had gone on to law school, launching a lucrative, high-powered career in corporate law. She'd never understood Ryan's dedication to his "little teaching job."

"But you ended up in business," Ryan cut in, retreating protectively. "A real career woman." The realization of how easily he could be swept away into the sultry depths of Maggie's misty green eyes burst over his mind. He looked around for Brandy, resolving to be more careful in the future.

Maggie stared at Ryan, stunned. *Where did that come from?* she wondered, feeling as if he'd just slapped her.

"Brandy, let's go," Ryan called. "I don't think we're going to see any 'gators today."

As he spoke, Maggie noticed a dark shadow gliding through the water beside a thin tree in the middle of the swamp. Its long head, saddled with bulging eye sockets, cut the water in a slim, straight line toward the bridge.

"Look, Brandy!" Maggie called. She grabbed Brandy's hand and pulled her away from her father and back to the edge of the bridge.

Brandy squealed with delight, clutching Maggie's hand tightly. Maggie looked over her shoulder. Ryan stood by her car, his face an expressionless mask.

Whatever had been between them for those few moments had evaporated as quickly as it had appeared, she realized.

The sounds of terror woke Ryan, rousing him from sleep automatically. He knew what was wrong. He'd been through it all before. Too many times.

"Brandy? Sweetheart?" he called as he stumbled down the dark hallway to his daughter's room. He crawled into the bed and hugged Brandy's small, shaking body. "I'm here," he comforted her, holding her tight. "Daddy's here."

"I dreamed—" Brandy cried, sobs choking out the words.

"I know, I know," Ryan whispered, rocking her back and forth.

"You won't ever leave me, will you, Daddy?" Brandy asked, her voice thick with tears.

"No, Brandy. You know I won't ever leave you."

"Mommy did."

Pain pricked along Ryan's nerves. He drew Brandy closer.

"I won't leave you, sweetheart. I promise. Cross my heart."

"And hope to die?"

"And hope to die," Ryan repeated.

He held her tight, knowing by the even rhythm of her breathing when she slept. But sleep eluded him, and he stared up at the ceiling, waiting for the soft rays of morning to light the room.

Would Brandy ever stop having nightmares? he wondered as he lay quietly, his daughter peaceful once more in his arms. He thought back to when the dreams had started, the night Delia had left.

Brandy had been three. So young, so impressionable. So unable to understand that her mother's sudden departure had nothing to do with her, in spite of her father's reassurances.

Brandy usually went for months without having the nightmare. Then it would come back suddenly, as forceful and terrifying as ever. Ryan could only console himself that the frequency of the nightmares was lessening as time went on. Brandy's pediatrician had assured him that eventually the dreams would subside completely.

She hadn't had the nightmare since she'd started seeing Maggie, he realized suddenly. There was usually a trigger to the episodes, he'd learned. Thinking back on the day before, he remembered their time at the movies, and stopping off at the bridge to watch for alligators.

When Maggie had dropped them off at home, Brandy had asked her to help her with her school play. All the kids' mothers were making costumes, Brandy had said. And so she wanted her special friend to help her.

Maggie had eagerly agreed.

Maybe, Ryan considered, Brandy wasn't quite as comfortable as she'd appeared with having Maggie substitute for her mother. Brandy rarely mentioned Delia, and it was difficult for Ryan to know how much hurt she might be hiding.

Pale light streaked through the divided panes of Brandy's bedroom window as Ryan fell asleep. The next thing he was aware of was his daughter poking his shoulder, calling his name.

"Daddy?" Brandy called, her voice close to his ear, her finger prodding insistently into his skin through his pajama top. "Wake up. Maggie's here."

Chapter Three

Ryan sleepily pulled himself up from Brandy's narrow twin bed, automatically reaching to rub the middle of his back with one hand. A night comforting Brandy never failed to leave him with aching muscles.

He yawned, staring at his daughter quizzically. Although he had no idea what time it was, he was sure it was early.

Too early for Maggie to be at his house.

"Come on, Daddy," Brandy said, tugging on his arm. She cocked her head to the side. "Did you forget Maggie said she was coming over this morning to help me with my costume for the play?" she asked.

He *had* forgotten. He glanced down at his blue striped pajamas.

"Tell her I'll be there in a minute," he told her as he stood, his joints rebelling as he stretched to his full height. "And get dressed," he instructed Brandy, noticing that she still wore her lace-edged flannel nightgown, bare toes peeping out below.

After treating his tired muscles to a shower that went by all too fast, and donning jeans and a thick, comfortable sweater, Ryan emerged into the hallway, tempted both by the rich aroma of coffee and the musical sounds of high-pitched laughter.

Turning the corner into the living room, Ryan found Brandy draped with a huge swatch of velvety forest green material while Maggie stood back, studying her, pins clenched between her teeth. A cup of steaming coffee rested on a nearby end table.

"Daddy!" Brandy squealed, spotting her father. "Look at me. I'm going to look like a real flower!"

Maggie turned and smiled tentatively at Ryan. She wasn't sure what to expect from him, especially after discovering that her arrival had woken him up.

"Hi," she said, removing the pins from her mouth. She could see Ryan had only recently emerged from a shower, his dark hair curling damply around the back of his sweater collar. He smelled lightly of musk—appealing and masculine. "I hope you don't mind that I took the liberty of making coffee in your kitchen. I brought doughnuts." She nodded to the dining room table, where a paper carton of glazed doughnuts waited.

"Actually, coffee sounds great right about now," Ryan told her, his voice softly neutral. "It was a long night. Thanks."

Maggie wondered what he was referring to, but hesitated to ask. The last time they'd strayed to a personal topic, she'd gotten her head bitten off. She wasn't in any hurry to repeat the experience.

She watched curiously, still unsure what Brandy's father's mood was on this early weekend morning. He meandered across the living room to the doughnuts, reaching into the box for one before turning toward the kitchen. Minutes later, he slumped down onto the living room couch with a steaming mug of fresh coffee, seemingly content to drink his coffee and eat his doughnut while observing the process spread out before him.

Maggie continued pinning material around Brandy, measuring and marking as she went. The intense certainty of Ryan's stare unnerved her. Turning once, she caught his eyes on her, then looked quickly away. Brandy continued chattering about her school play at a nonstop pace, easing what might otherwise have been an uncomfortable silence. Fumbling to move some of the pins, Maggie pricked the tip of one finger.

"Oh!" Maggie pulled back, poking her index finger against her tongue.

"Are you okay? Do you need a bandage?" Ryan asked, setting his mug down on the end table.

"No, no, I'm okay," Maggie told him, pressing the sore spot on her finger, her eyes averted from his.

Ryan frowned. He'd suspected Maggie was nervous, and he realized suddenly it was his presence that was causing the reaction. Had he been so unpleasant that being around him made her this uncomfortable?

He hadn't meant to make her so uneasy with him, only to keep her at a distance. A safe distance.

"I'm surprised you sew," he said, making an effort to strike up congenial conversation. As soon as Maggie's head turned to meet his gaze, he realized that he had, out of awkwardness, said the wrong thing.

"Really?" Maggie arched a dark brow. "Why is that? Can't we *career women* manage such domestic tasks?"

"I—"

"What did you think I was going to do when I said I was going to put Brandy's costume together? Go shopping?" Maggie demanded.

The outraged glow in her deep green eyes made Ryan want to laugh. When he gave in to the temptation, he witnessed the fire burn hotter in her gaze.

"You did, didn't you?" Maggie shook her head. "Well, I did go shopping. For material." Her glance shifted to Brandy and, noting the concern in the child's eyes, she forced herself to continue calmly. "See, this will be the stem of the flower." Maggie pointed to the green material pinned around Brandy's body. Gesturing to a pile of pink and purple cloth on the floor, she added, "And this is what I'll make the flower out of. It'll frame her face."

Brandy beamed as Maggie described the costume with growing enthusiasm, and Ryan felt a warmth seeping over his heart that he knew didn't come from the coffee. This was, on at least some level, the family dream that he'd yearned for once—seeing his daughter cared for by a loving woman. Whatever else he thought about Maggie and her high-powered career, it was clear that she cared about Brandy.

Maggie's words were lost on Ryan as he watched her, her eyes alight with enthusiasm as she held pieces of material and ribbon here and there, her face bright, her lips soft. He found his eyes traveling down to her slender shoulders, encased in a pearly white sweater over faded jeans that hugged her hips in a seductive embrace.

He pulled himself up short. Here he was, doing what he'd promised himself he wouldn't—indulging in his latent desire for Maggie Wells.

Standing, he walked into the dining room and poked another doughnut into his mouth. Brandy's next words rooted him where he stood.

"All the other kids have mothers to make their costumes," he heard Brandy saying, her voice small. "I told this one girl that I was going to have my grown-up friend Maggie make mine, and she said we were supposed to have our mommies do it. She said I couldn't be in the play if I didn't have a mommy to make my costume and that grown-up friends don't count."

Silence followed her remark for several seconds.

"And what did you say?" Maggie asked quietly.

Ryan pivoted to watch the scene. Maggie's face was as serious as Brandy's, her eyes filled with concern as she waited for the little girl to respond.

"I told her that she just wished she had a grown-up friend like you, and that you're going to make me something really neat to wear in the play," Brandy said. She bit her bottom lip when she finished and stared up at Maggie, round-eyed.

Maggie smiled, a slow spread upward of her lips.

"You know what?" Maggie asked. "You're right. Not everybody gets to be matched with a grown-up friend. But you did because you're special."

"I am?" Brandy grinned.

Maggie nodded. "Very special," she told Brandy, her expression becoming serious. "And you know what else? You *are* going to have a really neat costume. Now what about this bloom? Do you want mostly pink, or mostly purple?"

Ryan relaxed as he watched Maggie and Brandy concentrate on the costume, the moment of tension past. Maggie glanced up at him from across the room, a subtle question in her eyes. Ryan stared back, then allowed a trace of a smile to light his lips. Maggie smiled back.

He thought he felt his heart flip over.

By the next weekend, Maggie had convinced herself that her moment of connection with Ryan had been nothing more than imaginative thinking on her part, and she'd steeled herself to expect their normally distant relationship. Ryan seemed cool as usual when she picked Brandy up, and so she was surprised when he unexpectedly dropped by her house later in the day.

She had told him that she and Brandy would be spending the afternoon together there, but hadn't bothered to give him the details of what they would be doing, which included teaching Brandy how to make bread. After his reaction to her sewing Brandy's costume, she wasn't sure what to expect if he discovered that she enjoyed baking, too.

Intent on their creation of cinnamon swirl bread, Maggie didn't even notice Ryan's arrival until he came around to the screen door of the kitchen and rapped sharply. She'd been so engrossed in demonstrating to Brandy the technique of rolling up the cinnamon-filled loaves that she hadn't registered the sound of a car pulling up out front.

Ryan watched as Maggie turned at the sound of his knock, flour cascading down her buttoned-down yellow shirt onto her jeans. Another dusting of flour decorated one cheek. Dough clung to her fingers. She looked to her hands, then up again at Ryan, laughing self-consciously.

"Why don't you let yourself in?" she invited. Ryan stepped in, then almost retreated as Brandy ran toward him with dough-caked fingers.

"Look, Daddy. We're making bread," she announced proudly, pointing to the two loaf-filled pans atop the stove.

"I see," he nodded, smiling. He couldn't resist adding to Maggie, "So you bake, too?"

"Yes." Maggie stared at him, a defiant light in her eyes.

"A woman of many talents," Ryan murmured, meeting her gaze squarely.

"I'm so glad you finally recognize that," Maggie said, a flirtatious note in her voice. Then, as if embarrassed by the conversation, she switched to a more practical tone. "We're just now putting the bread up for its final rising," she explained. She wiped her floury hands on a blue-checked towel and turned on the water for Brandy. "Why don't you wash up?" she told the little girl.

When Brandy's hands were clean, Maggie took her turn at washing up before sitting down on a stool by the kitchen counter. She motioned to Ryan to take a stool beside her and he did while Brandy rushed after Romeo into the living room to play.

Ryan perched on the edge of the stool, glancing about the room. He wasn't sure what had come over him to bring him to Maggie's house. He'd originally intended only to stop off at the grocery store for milk. Suddenly he'd found himself in front of Maggie's house, almost as if someone else had driven him there.

"What brings you here?" Maggie queried.

Ryan faced her, catching the curiosity in her eyes as she asked the question. He was tempted to confess he felt the same way—uncertain and bemused. And enchanted by the red-haired beauty he couldn't get out of his mind. She was so close, and she smelled so sweet. The swipe of flour on her cheek mesmerized him. He wanted to reach out and wipe it away, to feel her soft skin—

He swallowed. "I was just in the neighborhood," he managed. He smiled at her disbelieving stare. "Okay, I confess. I wanted to see where you lived."

Maggie eyed Ryan as she cupped her chin in her palms and leaned her elbows on the counter. He seemed nervous, appealingly vulnerable. And more honest and open than she'd ever seen him. She was fascinated.

"Why?"

"I don't know," he admitted. A wave of relief swept over him at the confession. His eyes stayed on Maggie, waiting for her reaction.

Maggie straightened, laughing, softly at first, then louder, and Ryan joined in. His laugh was deliciously deep and warm, Maggie thought to herself. She found herself wishing she could hear it more often.

"I've never seen you laugh before," Maggie noted when her mirth subsided. "I didn't know you ever laughed," she teased. Then, more seriously, she added, "You know that I really care about your daughter. Brandy is a wonderful child. I hope by now you realize that I have her best interests at heart."

He was silent a moment. She did have Brandy's best interests at heart, he knew. He'd already thought it to himself a number of times. But putting the thought into words and expressing it came hard for Ryan. He'd cared for Brandy completely by himself for three years. He'd never realized when he entered her in the women's outreach program how deep an effect that decision would have on Brandy's life. Or how profoundly it would also affect him.

That decision had brought Maggie into their lives. And nothing had been the same since.

"Yes," he said slowly, feeling the tension ease in his chest as he voiced his thoughts aloud. "I know that you're good for her. She looks forward to her times with you. It's good for her to have someone to do things like this with," he said, waving an arm at the loaves on the counter. "Her mother never bakes bread," he added.

"That doesn't make her a bad person any more than it makes me a good person," Maggie noted, feeling herself on unsteady ground as always during the rare occasions when the topic of Ryan's former wife came up.

"True," Ryan said, "but there's more to it than that." He stared pensively at Maggie's kitchen floor, studying the pattern of tiny blue flowers and squares in the tiles.

"Why doesn't Brandy see her mother?" Maggie asked impulsively.

Ryan's eyes shuttered immediately. "Like I said before, her mother lives out of state." He clearly didn't wish to elaborate.

Maggie wasn't satisfied, but she was afraid to go further and lose the fragile camaraderie they'd only just found.

She decided to drop the subject of Brandy's mother. For now. "Why did you really come over here today?" she asked softly.

Ryan relaxed, and his eyes met hers with openness again. "I really did want to see where you lived," he said. "And I wanted to say..." He hesitated. Then, as if the words came hard for him, he finished quickly. "I wanted to say I was sorry that things got off on the wrong foot between us."

"Really?" Maggie all but dropped her jaw at the apology.

Ryan looked appealingly sheepish. "Yes, really. I'm not an ogre, you know."

Maggie recalled her first conversation with Emma, in which her friend had said she made Ryan sound like exactly that. He definitely didn't look anything like an ogre now.

A tremble of warmth spun up her spine. No, he didn't look like an ogre at all. Just the opposite, in fact. With his dark hair and piercing eyes, set amidst a chiseled face, he easily qualified as handsome. But it was the combination of those same startling looks with this unexpected gentleness and humor that made the difference—that made Maggie's heart beat double time.

"I know," she agreed at last.

Ryan grinned, and Maggie beamed back. He was struck anew by the glory of her smile. She positively glowed, with her soft, inviting lips and her sweet, sparkling eyes.

He noticed the dusting on her cheek again and this time couldn't resist. "You know you have a spot of flour right here—" He picked up a napkin from the basket on the counter and lifted it to her smooth skin.

She grew very still under his ministration. He could feel her breath against his hand. Neither of them spoke. She felt warm and soft beneath his touch. Slowly, as he wiped off the small streak of flour, an ache formed inside him. He didn't want to stop there, with a mere touch. It wasn't enough.

He wanted to kiss those soft, inviting lips. He wanted to make those sweet, sparkling eyes close in passion.

He wanted *Maggie.*

Maggie sat motionless, spellbound, as Ryan moved the napkin across her cheek, the gesture as gentle as a caress. Heat coiled up from a secret well deep within her. She didn't know what was happening, only that she couldn't—wouldn't—stop it. Her body felt limp with unaccustomed need as he leaned toward her, closer, until there was nothing between them but a breath, and then—

"Maggie!"

Ryan pulled back sharply, his blood pounding wildly, as Brandy ran into the kitchen and flung herself at Maggie.

"Don't leave," she cried against Maggie's chest as Maggie leaned down to hold her.

"What?" Maggie asked, confused by Brandy's sudden fear, bewildered by the kiss she had almost shared with Ryan. Her heart still pattered irregularly inside her chest.

"I followed Romeo into your room," Brandy said, breathing heavily between the words. "I saw your suitcase all packed with your clothes. Where are you going?"

"Brandy, I'm just going on a business trip on Monday," Maggie explained, rubbing Brandy's back as she spoke, anxious to reassure her, forgetting Ryan for a second. While Brandy's mother remained a mystery in many respects, Maggie was sure of one thing—the woman had caused deep scars in the daughter she'd left behind. "Don't worry. I'll just be gone a few days. I'm attending a conference in Baltimore."

"Really?" Brandy asked, her small face still set in worry lines.

"Really," Maggie assured her. "Would you like me to call you while I'm gone?" Brandy nodded. "Okay, then I will," Maggie promised.

Looking up then, Maggie was taken aback sharply by the change in Ryan. The gentleness, openness and warmth of a few moments before were gone, replaced by the cool reserve she knew too well. Had she imagined the laughter? The desire? The near kiss? How could it all disappear so quickly?

"Why don't I take Brandy home, since I'm here," Ryan suggested, pulling his daughter away from her.

Maggie frowned, shaken by both Brandy's fears and Ryan's reaction. "The bread—" she started to say.

"It's getting late, anyway," he said. "Come on, Brandy." He prodded the little girl toward the screen door, and with a quick wave of her small hand, they were gone.

Maggie leaned against the counter again. She could hear the roar of Ryan's engine as he started up the blue sedan and the gentle whir as he drove away. Then there was nothing but silence, and the one question that kept ringing in her mind.

What in the world had just happened?

Maggie stared out the window of her office onto the busy street below. She didn't notice the cars or the shoppers and tourists who crowded the downtown Charleston sidewalks. Her thoughts were filled with Ryan, and had been for months, she had at last admitted to herself.

The realization had come to Maggie while she was in Baltimore, alone in a hotel suite, its luxury lost on her. After so many hotel suites and so many conferences, they all looked alike. She'd tried to bury herself in paperwork during the long quiet evenings alone in the hotel, as she usually did, but found herself repeatedly laying her reports aside and thinking of Brandy's father. She'd called Brandy a couple of times, and the brief exchanges with Ryan before he put Brandy on the phone had only made matters worse.

Now, as she had then, she replayed in her mind those moments in her kitchen, remembering how she and Ryan had laughed together. How they'd nearly kissed.

She thought back even further to the few moments of rapport they had shared on the country bridge, to the smile of gratitude he'd shot her the day she'd measured Brandy for her costume.

Why didn't they have more moments like that? Why did something always spoil it? No sooner would he warm up to her than he would draw back.

She was amazed at how intrigued she was by him. No matter how grouchy he pretended to be, she knew he wasn't. He was a loving, caring father, generous with his time, devoted to his daughter's well-being.

But when it came to Maggie, something held him back, kept him from unleashing his true self. Only on those occasions when he seemed to forget himself did he relax and open up.

Now, on Maggie's first morning back at work, her thoughts were still consumed by Ryan, in spite of the mound of mail and reports waiting in neat stacks atop her desk. Chin resting on her fist, she stared out the window. In her mind's eye she saw Ryan, his broad shoulders tapering down to a lean waist and long legs, rich chestnut hair, sparkling azure eyes and a wide mouth that could, when he allowed it, spread into a deliciously intoxicating smile.

"Maggie?"

Maggie drew her hand down quickly and turned toward the door to her office.

"Mike, good morning," she said, slightly embarrassed as she shifted determinedly back to business. Mike Roberts, the district supervisor, sat down in the cushioned chair across from her desk.

"And how was Baltimore?" he asked.

"Busy," Maggie answered automatically. "I'll have a report for you by tomorrow, but I can fill you in on a few of the conference highlights now if you'd like," she offered, struggling to focus her mind on her recent trip.

Mike Roberts leaned against the straight back of the office chair and shook his head.

"I think I can wait for that," he said. "What I really came in here for was to warn you about what you're about to hear on the office grapevine. I wanted you to hear it from me first, so you'd know it was true."

Maggie smiled at him quizzically as he leaned forward over her desk.

"I'm happy to tell you I've put your name in for the District Achiever Award this year," he told her. "Your work has been excellent and you deserve it."

Maggie's eyes widened. "Mike, thank you," she said at last. "I don't know what to say. Thank you."

"Don't thank me," he said, rising. "You earned it." He walked to the door. "The winner will be announced at the company awards banquet in June, as usual."

The upcoming banquet would be held in a downtown Charleston luxury hotel. Nominees and company officials would be attending from all over the district.

"I'll be there," Maggie said, smiling widely as he left.

She leaned back in her chair. District Achiever was the top honor bestowed annually on one employee out of all those nominated by the company's various district offices. She'd hoped to be nominated for it eventually, of course, but this year? She hadn't expected it yet.

What would Ryan think? she suddenly wondered, bursting to tell someone. But she knew then that she wouldn't mention it to Brandy's father.

Maggie worked all day Saturday, catching up on some of the reports that had piled up during her absence. She didn't have plans with Brandy for the weekend, but after coming home and eating a quick supper, she couldn't resist giving her a call to see if they might do something the next day. Although the women's outreach program only required she see Brandy twice a month, Maggie found she missed the little girl on the weekends they didn't get together.

No doubt about it. She'd gotten attached to Brandy but good. As for Brandy's father and how she felt about him—well, she needed to stop thinking about him. That was all there was to that!

Maggie dialed, shoving off the uncomfortable thoughts of Ryan.

"Hello?" Brandy answered.

"Hi, sweetheart! It's Maggie. I just wanted to see what you were doing tomorrow. I thought we might have a picnic at the park. You want to ask your daddy if that would be all right?"

"My daddy's sick," Brandy said. She hesitated. "He's asleep. He's been sleeping almost all day."

Maggie picked up the thread of anxiety in the girl's small voice. "What's wrong with him?"

"I don't know. He's just really sick. He won't get out of bed, and he's really hot. I don't know if I can go tomorrow. I don't want to leave my daddy alone." She sounded upset.

"Are you by yourself?" Maggie asked quickly. "Just you and your daddy?"

"Uh-huh. I've been watching TV all day, in Daddy's room." The little girl's voice trembled. "Maggie, will you come over? I don't have anybody to put me to bed and read me my story. And Daddy said he needed some medicine, too, but he said we didn't have any. And then he went to sleep again."

"Oh, Brandy, of course I'll come over! And I'll bring some medicine. I'll be right there!"

Maggie told her goodbye and hung up, immediately rushing to gather her purse and car keys. She wasn't sure, but she could guess that Ryan had a case of the flu that had been going around, and even if she didn't feel quite comfortable playing Florence Nightingale for him, she certainly couldn't leave Brandy there alone and afraid.

After a quick stop at the drugstore, Maggie arrived at the Conner house. She rang the bell and called out that it was her so Brandy would open the door. The little girl led her back to her father's bedroom—a bastion of masculinity with a checked brown-and-green comforter and heavy wooden furniture. A sitcom played softly on a TV in the corner.

Ryan lay on the bed, a sheet pulled up in a messy tangle around his waist. His chest, sprinkled with dark hairs, was bare. He opened his eyes and blinked in surprise when he saw her.

"Hi," Maggie said, feeling incredibly embarrassed. She glanced over her shoulder, wondering where Brandy had run off to the moment they'd reached her father's room. "I don't mean to intrude. I spoke to Brandy a little while ago. She said you were sick, and she asked me to come over to read her bedtime story and bring you some medicine."

"She did?" Ryan's voice came out scratchy and weak.

"She said you were asleep, and she sounded pretty upset." Maggie juggled the bag from the drugstore from one arm to the other. Along with some aspirin and flu remedies, she'd picked up juice and soup. With her free hand, she held on to the doorframe as if it were a life preserver. She tried to concentrate on Ryan's face and not look at his bare chest, or the muscular curve of his shoulders and arms. It was a difficult task. "Can I do something for you?"

Ryan tried to focus on what was happening. He felt as if he had a hundred jackhammers operating inside his head at once. Most of the day had been a fevered blur. He'd woken up sick, and Brandy had managed for herself all day, eating jelly sandwiches and watching TV in his room. He'd been aware of it all only vaguely.

He was very aware of Maggie, however. She looked like an angel, a beautiful angel in faded jeans that hugged the slender curve of her thighs and a lightweight green sweater that outlined her breasts. Her heart-shaped face was gentle with concern.

He knew he felt like hell warmed over, and he had to look worse.

He didn't even begin to have the strength to analyze why that bothered him so. Instead, he used what energy he had to sit up and swing his pajama-clad legs over the side of the bed.

"I'm fine," he said as he stood. He hadn't eaten all day, and the lack of medication had left his fever unchecked. Dizzy and weak, he felt his legs wobble. Then his knees began to buckle—

"Ryan!" Maggie dropped the bag from the drugstore and dashed across the room. Sliding her arm around his waist, she helped him back onto the bed. The intimacy of the action struck her immediately, and her pulse revved. Despite his obvious weakness at the moment, he had a strong body, hard and muscular. He was a big man and somehow, naked from the waist up, he seemed even bigger, even more impressive. Even more desirable.

Tingles swept to every nerve ending in Maggie's body with the speed of fire across a dry prairie. She felt ablaze with something unfamiliar and frightening.

She swallowed, hard, and took a step back, struggling to distance herself from Ryan. He was sick and disheveled. And he still managed to put her nerves into a panic, her senses into a spin.

She went on the offensive out of self-protectiveness. "What do you think you're doing, trying to get up?" she scolded. "You lie down and don't move. No wonder Brandy was so worried!"

Ryan pulled the sheet up to his waist and rested his pounding head on his pillow. If possible, he felt even worse than before. The brief exertion of trying to stand up had sapped the small bit of strength he'd had left.

Maggie putting her slender, soft arm around his waist had him frustrated beyond belief. She smelled good enough to eat and she looked like heaven on earth. And she was practically in his bed. He had an incredible, inexplicable urge to ravish her madly—and he was completely incapable of doing anything about it. "I'm fine," he barked in irritation.

"Oh, really?" Maggie sat down on the edge of the bed as primly as possible, making sure not to rub up against the long legs Ryan had slid beneath the sheet. She reached for his forehead and pressed her hand against it for a moment. She grew instantly more worried. "You feel like you're on fire, and you can't even stand up."

Ryan gazed up at her, and she saw how fever-bright his eyes were. And she saw something else. Something unspoken, but real. It was awareness, crackling and alive.

Her mouth went dry. She jerked her hand back.

"Have you had a flu shot?" she demanded.

"I hate needles," Ryan admitted. He coughed. "Brandy's had one, though."

"So have I. Next year you should get one, too. I'm afraid it's too late for you this year." Maggie stood up briskly. "Tell me where your thermometer is. I want to take your temperature, then I'll put Brandy to bed for you."

Ryan told her where she could find the item in question, and Maggie went off to look for it. She found Brandy in the hallway, coming out of her own room. She'd changed into her nightgown.

"Is my daddy okay?"

Maggie bent to wrap the little girl in a warm hug. "He's going to be fine. Why don't you go climb into your bed and I'll be there in a minute, just as soon as I get something for your daddy."

Brandy padded off to her room obediently while Maggie retrieved the thermometer and returned to

Ryan's room. She'd brought a glass with her from the kitchen and set it down—along with the bag from the drugstore—on the nightstand.

Taking a deep breath, she sat down beside Ryan on the bed again. "Here." She poked the digital thermometer between his lips in a no-nonsense fashion, then studied her watch with unnecessary intensity. She was afraid if she didn't, she'd end up staring at his chest again.

Moments ticked by.

"Mmmmpph!" Ryan made impatient noises around the thermometer. Maggie looked up.

"Hush!" she warned him. She hesitated, then gave him a shy smile. "Just one more minute."

It spiraled to Ryan's chest, that smile. Like a heat-seeking missile, it found his heart and wrapped right around it.

He felt strangely comforted and let his lids droop shut, giving in to the exhaustion and pounding inside his head. The vision of Maggie with her cloud of red hair and gentle emerald eyes danced around the edges of his mind as he began to drift off.

Maggie removed the thermometer from Ryan's mouth and was shocked when she read it. Snapping her worried gaze back to him, she saw that he'd turned his head to the side and was resting limply against the pillow, eyes closed.

Digging into the bag from the drugstore, she unloaded the juice and medicine. She removed two fever-reducing capsules and nudged Ryan. "You have to take these," she said softly. His lashes fluttered in response and he stared feverishly up at her. "Here." She moved to prop another pillow behind his head and then gently placed the medicine into his mouth. Her fingers brushed over his lips as she drew away.

The connection yielded a sharp zap that sent Maggie scurrying for cover. She busied herself pouring him a cup of juice, then held it to his mouth. He drank a few sips, then sank back, his eyes closing once again. *Had that brief charge of awareness really happened? And if it had, had she been the only one to feel it?*

She watched him sleep for a moment, then switched off the TV in the corner and hurried off to take care of Brandy.

A short time later, with the little girl tucked into bed, Maggie crept back into Ryan's room and found him still sleeping. She again sat on the edge of the bed and felt his forehead. If anything, he burned hotter than before.

She chewed her lip. The fever-reducing medication wasn't working. Maggie stared at him, troubled.

She couldn't leave him this way. She wasn't a nurse, but she knew what her mother would do.

Maggie headed for the kitchen, her mind made up. She found a large bowl in the cupboard and filled it with tepid water. In the bathroom, she picked up two thick, colorful washcloths.

She sat beside Ryan in the darkened room, the glow of his bedside lamp spilling out over him, settling shadows into his chiseled profile. Setting the bowl on the nightstand, Maggie dunked the cloths into the water.

Withdrawing the first one, she wrung it out, folded it and draped it across his forehead. His lashes trembled briefly, then he opened his eyes and stared up at Maggie. He started to speak, then began to cough.

"Shh." Maggie hushed him, and when he stopped coughing, he was quiet, watching her as she wrung out the second cloth over the bowl. "I'm worried about your temperature," she whispered. "You're too hot."

Gently she began to bathe him. Starting with his face, she massaged him, cooling the blood brought to the surface as the water evaporated on his skin. His eyes drifted shut again as she moved from one cheek to the other, then to his neck and chest, then to his stomach, rewetting the cloth as she went.

The process was achingly intimate. Maggie became familiar with every dip and curve of his body from the waist up—the hard swells of his well-developed chest, the taut plane of his stomach, the trim line of his waist.

Slowly she felt his body cooling beneath her touch, while her own insides heated with her reaction to touching him in this way. The ministration was private, nurturing and seductive. As she moved the cloth over his firm abdomen, the kernel of fire inside her swelled, exploding outward in quivers of desire as she brushed along the waistline of his pajama bottoms.

She looked up suddenly, a tickle of awareness warning her, and found Ryan watching her once more. She felt herself blushing in what she knew from experience would be a fiery show of splendor. "You're awake," she blurted, embarrassed, jerking the cloth from his stomach and dropping it into the bowl.

"Don't stop," Ryan said softly, too weak to censor his thoughts. He didn't want her to stop touching him. Rather, he wanted to drag her down beside him and make love to her. Unfortunately, he felt as helpless as a newborn.

Maggie's nerves bounced erratically as she stared at Ryan. *Don't stop.* Was he teasing? Confused? *Serious?* "I—I think you're going to be fine now. Your skin is much cooler." Reaching up, she removed the cloth from his forehead. She noticed that her hands shook slightly. "How do you feel?"

"Like somebody hit me over the head with a sledgehammer."

Maggie stood up. "I bet you haven't had anything to eat all day, have you?" Ryan shook his head. "I'm going to fix you some soup before I leave."

She picked up the bag she'd brought with her, along with the bowl and cloths, and headed for the kitchen, practically stumbling in her anxiousness to escape. A short while later, she reappeared with a bowl of chicken noodle soup and a glass of water.

Ryan managed to prop himself up on his own, shoving another pillow behind his back, and Maggie sat down beside him. Placing the water on the nightstand, she dipped a spoon into the soup and began to feed him.

For a split second, Ryan thought of objecting, then didn't, surprising no one more than himself. The truth was, he was enjoying Maggie's ministrations. Far too much.

When he'd obediently consumed the soup and water, Maggie brought him another cup of juice. "Don't forget to take your medicine in the morning," she instructed. She wondered what it would be like to be there in the morning, to wake up beside him, to be his wife—

She stood abruptly. *What was she thinking?*

"Thank you."

He was grateful, of course. And that was *all*, she warned herself. Whatever else she might have imagined was just that—her imagination, working overtime. She forced a shrug. "It was no big deal."

Then she fled.

Brandy let go of Maggie's hand and skated in a circle around her, laughing at Maggie's worried face, then grabbing her hand again. Maggie reached for the side rail as they slowed down together and clopped onto the carpet outside the rink.

"You're dangerous," Maggie accused between gasps of air. "I can see I'm going to have to start doing aerobics if I'm going to keep up with you."

Two weekends had passed since she'd last been with Brandy. Ryan had asked her to pick Brandy up at a friend's house where she'd been at a sleepover, so Maggie had not seen him since the day he'd been sick. She felt as if she had, though, from the many times he had intruded unexpectedly into her thoughts of late. Just his voice over the phone as she'd scheduled the skating date had sent warm streaks through her bloodstream, frightening her a little in their uninvited intensity.

She tried to shake off thoughts of him as she plopped down on a wooden bench beside his daughter.

"I want you to come to my house for dinner," Brandy said as she unlaced her skates. "My dad's making lasagna. He said there'd be lots for everybody. Come. Please."

Maggie looked up from her own tangled laces and stared at Brandy. The little girl held her foot out to Maggie, who leaned down and tugged off the skate.

"Are you sure this was your father's idea?" Maggie asked, watching Brandy's face closely.

"He said so," Brandy said firmly, and carried her skates to the rental counter.

Maggie thought about the low-calorie frozen dinner she had planned, along with an evening of television or reading. Then she imagined Ryan, tall and lean, puttering over noodles and tomato sauce in his kitchen.

The image brought a smile to her lips—and a flutter to her heart. Rising, she followed Brandy to the counter. Plunking down her skates, she took Ryan's daughter's hand. "Let's go," Maggie said.

Chapter Four

"Let's stop here a minute," Maggie said to Brandy suddenly, swerving her silver sports car to the right and pulling to a stop in front of a small florist's shop. "I'll get something for the table."

Brandy tagged along behind her as she entered the store.

"Help me choose the flowers," Maggie suggested. "Then they'll be from both of us."

Brandy studied the refrigerated display cases carefully, walking back and forth with lips pursed, as if deciding a matter of great import.

"Let's get these," she decided at last, pointing to a tall vase of assorted spring blooms of iris, daffodils and tulips. "We have these in our yard, but Daddy never lets me pick them. I did once, and he got mad."

Maggie laughed as she removed the flowers from the case and brought them to the salesclerk.

Back in the car, the little girl chattered without stopping, gingerly holding the vase out in front of herself all the way to her house. All Maggie could think about was that Ryan had invited her to dinner. Perhaps this meant that their tentative truce was back on. She refused to let herself think it could be anything more.

Nothing would make Maggie happier than to see the truce become permanent. She longed to retrieve those peaceful moments when she and Ryan had talked and enjoyed each other's company. But she couldn't help remembering those fleeting moments when she'd thought she'd seen desire in his deep blue gaze....

When they pulled up at the house, Brandy handed the arrangement to Maggie and skipped excitedly up the walk, opening the door and disappearing inside, leaving Maggie to let herself in.

She stopped in the doorway and peered around hesitantly. Ryan was nowhere to be seen. Lifting her nose, Maggie breathed in the unmistakably pungent aroma of Italian food coming from down the hall.

Rather than waiting for Brandy to reappear, Maggie resolutely headed for the warm light of the kitchen. She found Ryan peering into an open hot oven, where he was patting down foil over a large casserole dish, his hands protected by huge yellow mitts. Maggie was silent, watching the muscles move in his arms beneath his short sleeves as he rearranged the foil cover.

He shut the oven and turned, his eyes widening upon seeing her.

"Maggie. I didn't know you were there."

His azure eyes took in the flowers, and his brow crinkled slightly, but he didn't comment on them. Maggie set them down on the beige countertop.

"Brandy went to her room or something. I'm not really sure," she said. "We brought these for the table." She fingered a piece of trailing greenery nervously.

Now Ryan raised an eyebrow.

"You did?" he asked.

"Yes," Maggie responded, smiling at his apparent surprise. "I suppose you think I have no manners." When he didn't say anything, she added, "Maybe I should check if they need water."

She knew full well the arrangement didn't need any water, but busied herself with inspecting the vase, anyway. She detected something in his expression that she couldn't quite define. She almost thought he seemed a little bewildered.

"Brandy picked them out." Noticing his continued bemused look, she laughed lightly. "Don't worry. These aren't from your yard."

"Oh, no, that's not what I was thinking," Ryan replied. He shook his head, appearing amused, and removed the thick yellow oven mitts that he wore. "But I'm glad to hear it, anyway."

"I'll just put these flowers on the table," Maggie offered. Ryan was still staring at her with an odd expression as she brushed by him toward the dining room. Maggie placed the vase in the middle of the rectangular oak table, noticing as she did the two plastic plates set side by side.

Two plates. Two place settings. Plastic.

Maggie swung around. Ryan was watching her quizzically from the open doorway of the kitchen, the light behind him casting a soft glow around his chestnut hair. She could feel herself blushing hot, the horrible curse that she always blamed on her red hair.

Brandy ran up behind her father and grabbed him about the waist.

"Daddy! I told Maggie it would be all right with you if she came for dinner, okay?" Brandy said, hugging him. She smiled up at her father, then turned innocently to Maggie. "You're staying, aren't you?"

"Well..." Maggie began, but the words to relieve her from the painfully embarrassing situation failed her.

"Of course she's staying," Ryan said, smoothly assuming control of the conversation. "We have plenty and we'd love to have her stay for dinner."

The laughter in his eyes remained, but his gaze on Maggie was warm, soothing. The kindness in his eyes only confused her more.

"That's what I said," Brandy told him. "I told her you said there was lots for everybody."

"I'm sorry," Maggie said finally, feeling the blush receding at last from her hot cheeks. "I didn't mean to intrude. I must have misunderstood. I had the impression that this was your idea, Ryan. I can go. I'll go."

Maggie headed for the living room, determined to escape as quickly as possible. She felt a firm grip on her arm.

"Stay."

It was one word, but it was the one word she had wanted to hear Ryan say. She turned slowly to face him.

"I want you to," he added. "Don't be embarrassed."

His hand seemed to scorch into her skin where he touched her. He smelled like tomato sauce and oregano, with a touch of musk.

"I'm not embarrassed," Maggie returned. She smiled ruefully. "Well, not too badly embarrassed, anyway."

"Then you'll stay," he said.

"I'll stay," she agreed, and Ryan released her arm and directed her out the sliding glass doors onto the back patio. Settling her in a long, padded lawn chair on the deck, he turned back to the house.

"Relax," he advised. "I'm sure you're worn-out from skating. I've been skating with Brandy myself." He smiled at her knowingly, sending a new rush of heat to her cheeks. "I'll let you know when dinner is ready."

Maggie started to offer to help, then stopped as he shut the glass door behind him. He didn't really seem to want her help, and anyway, it was easier to recover from her embarrassment with a few moments alone, she decided. She leaned back against the soft chair. The early evening was pleasant with the spring warmth that was characteristic of Charleston.

Several minutes later, Brandy burst out the door and ran to sit on the edge of Maggie's chair. She grinned, the expression lighting her face with sweet appeal.

"I'm sorry," Brandy said.

"Did your father tell you to say that?" Maggie asked suspiciously.

Brandy smiled, her lips curving with mischievous honesty. "Yes," she admitted. Then she continued quickly, "I didn't mean to say that Daddy exactly invited you. I just meant he wouldn't mind. And he doesn't—see?"

Maggie laughed at the childish logic.

"You're not mad at me, are you, Maggie?" Brandy asked, her face suddenly serious.

"No, of course not," Maggie assured her. "It's okay." She ruffled Brandy's hair. "And lasagna's my favorite dish, anyway."

"I love you, Maggie," Brandy said, and she leaned up and put her arms around Maggie's neck. Maggie felt tears prick her eyes.

"I love you, too, Brandy," she heard herself confess. A lump swelled in her throat. She hadn't thought of her feelings in those terms, she realized. But it was true nonetheless. She loved Brandy. Her feelings for the little girl's complex father, however, were more difficult to define. More difficult—and more frightening....

Maggie stared out at the newly green spring grass on the back lawn, frowning. Hadn't she vowed to keep her mind from straying onto that subject?

Brandy hugged Maggie tighter, then, after one last squeeze, jumped up and ran off toward her tree house to show Maggie how she could climb. Maggie settled comfortably into her chaise to watch.

Finally Ryan returned, balancing two glasses of red wine in his hands. Leaning down, he handed one to

Maggie before turning back to close the sliding glass door.

"Thanks," Maggie said. She felt her senses come alive in Ryan's presence, suddenly aware of every beat of her heart, every tingle of her skin. She sipped from her glass, and tried to focus on Brandy across the lawn.

Ryan pulled up a deck chair and sat down beside Maggie, watching her profile, wondering if she was still embarrassed. Although he'd ordered Brandy to apologize for placing her in such an awkward situation, the truth was that he couldn't be happier that she was staying for dinner.

"I'm glad you're here," Ryan said, voicing his thoughts.

Maggie turned slowly to face him, her eyes dark and questioning.

"Are you?" she asked, her gaze searching his, suspiciously.

He nodded.

"Thanks." She smiled a little warily. "I have to admit, I feel kind of silly about, well, about what happened when I first got here."

Ryan laughed and shook his head. "Don't. I'm glad you're staying for dinner." Cocking his head slightly, he added, "I only wish it had been my idea."

He detected a return of the enchanting pinkening of her cheeks he'd seen earlier, when Maggie had discovered that he didn't know Brandy had invited her to dinner. He remembered, too, the shy blushes that had swept over her the day he'd been sick. The knowledge that a successful, beautiful woman such as Maggie Wells still possessed the innocence behind a blush delighted him. He resisted the urge to reach out and run his fingers lightly along her cheeks, to absorb some of her soft warmth into the heat that was building inside him as he watched her.

"Are you sure there's not something I can do to help with dinner?" Maggie asked.

"No." Ryan shook his head again. "This is my treat. It's my chance to pay you back for helping me when I was sick, remember?"

Maggie went even redder, remembering that sponge bath and the wayward path of her thoughts. "That was nothing," she demurred.

"On the contrary," Ryan protested. "I'm not used to having anyone around to help out like that."

"I know what you mean," Maggie agreed, eager to change the subject before he could guess her train of thought. "That's why you should always have flu shots," she chided. "The illness is worse than the needle. You have to get over your fears."

"I'm working on it," Ryan said, his stare intense.

The blaze of warmth from his eyes shot a sudden wave of electric excitement over Maggie. She wondered if they were still talking about needles.

She sipped her wine, swallowing its cool sweetness gratefully.

"I hope so," she said.

He smiled broadly then, and she smiled back. A deep sense of happiness filled her, though she couldn't have explained why.

"I better check dinner," Ryan said.

Moments later he called Brandy and Maggie inside. The change in the dining room struck Maggie immediately. Gone were the plastic plates and paper napkins. Three plates in gleaming silver and white china lay on the table, surrounded by white cloth napkins, shining silverware and sparkling clear glasses of ice water. Goblets of red wine stood by two of the plates. Maggie's spring blooms provided a splash of bright color in the center.

"The table is beautiful," Maggie told Ryan as he held a match to a single white candle that stood in a brass holder beside the flowers. The knowledge that he considered her worthy of such an obviously special setting melted her insides.

Looking into his eyes, she saw a golden gleam in his blue depths. The gleam seemed to shoot right into her body and envelop her heart with joy and anticipation.

"We're having dinner with a candle?" Brandy gushed.

Ryan smiled and nodded, still looking at Maggie as he said, "We have to make a deserving setting for our flowers."

Maggie smiled back at him.

I've never seen him like this, she thought to herself. *I wonder what caused the change in him?*

Ryan pulled out a chair for Maggie, and then for Brandy, before bringing out the large dish of lasagna along with a crisp green salad and hot crusty French bread. Sitting across the table from Ryan, Maggie ate in nervous excitement, barely even tasting the meal. She knew only that the lasagna was fragrant with herbs and tomatoes, the salad crunched freshly and the bread dissolved in her mouth. And Ryan's eyes glowed with soft desire, adding an aura of subtle bewitchment to the evening.

"It's wonderful," Maggie told him, finally slowing the pace of her nerves enough to savor the meal's taste. "I'm impressed with your domestic prowess."

"Daddy cooks a lot," Brandy told Maggie.

"I like to cook," Ryan agreed. "It's something of a hobby, which is convenient since it's also a necessity."

"Maggie makes bread," Brandy piped in. "You guys should make dinner together. Maggie could make the bread and you could make the rest of it, Daddy."

Maggie smiled at Brandy.

"Well, we'll see about that," Maggie said, beginning to feel a little flushed again by Brandy's rapid progression. She glanced across the table at Ryan, but he didn't seem perturbed by his daughter's suggestion. His eyes shone into Maggie's, the yellow candlelight in the darkening room bringing a peaceful composure to his face. Maggie had never seen him so relaxed.

She felt her own nerves mellowing, whether from the magnetic spell of Ryan or from the intoxicating sweetness of the wine, she wasn't sure. It was easy, almost too easy, to bask in his unexpected attention.

"I think that's a great idea," she heard him saying.

She glanced up at him in confusion.

"You and I collaborating on a meal, like Brandy was saying," Ryan explained.

"Oh, yes." She smiled. "That would be wonderful." He smiled back.

After the meal was finished, Maggie insisted on helping Ryan clear the table and wash the dishes while Brandy watched television in the living room.

"I hope you didn't mind about all this," Maggie said as she laid the damp towel on the counter when the last dish was dried and put away.

"What, about having you to dinner?" Ryan asked. He moved closer, until he was inches from her face, watching her in the fluorescent brightness of the kitchen. "No," he murmured softly, "I didn't mind." He reached up and touched a lock of her shoulder-length auburn hair and pushed it back behind her neck. In the bold light, the soul behind her eyes seemed bared to him. He saw need and wonder—and a desire that found an echo inside himself.

"Will you read me my bedtime story, Maggie?" Brandy called as she scampered into the kitchen. Ryan drew his hand back quickly as his daughter entered the room.

"I'd love to," Maggie agreed, oddly relieved that they had been interrupted. The moment had seemed unreal, like a dream. A dream she wasn't sure she was ready for. And yet, she couldn't squelch a feeling of disappointment.

She followed Brandy through the living room and down the hall to her pretty pink room filled with stuffed animals and dolls. Already having donned her gown, Brandy crawled into bed and lay back expectantly. Maggie picked up a book from her nightstand. "This one?" she asked.

Brandy nodded, and Maggie opened the children's adventure story to a chapter indicated by a thin blue bookmark. In the soft light of Brandy's lamp, she read. Brandy listened quietly, her eyes slowly closing. Near the end of the chapter, Maggie could see that she had fallen asleep. She replaced the book on the table and leaned forward to kiss Brandy's cheek, then switched off the lamp and turned to the door.

Ryan's tall form stood like a shadow in the open doorway against the light that radiated down the hall from the living room. He was quiet, simply watching Maggie with his daughter.

"You do that very well," he whispered as she reached the door. He moved just enough for her to skim past him, then followed her back to the living room.

Maggie looked around for her purse in the gently filtered lamplight, confused about where she'd left it when she came in, unable to think straight under Ryan's eyes. She couldn't see him, but she knew he was behind her, watching her.

"Where's my purse?" she asked aloud, then spotted it on an end table.

"You don't have to go," Ryan said behind her. "I don't want you to."

She turned to face him, and he placed a warm hand over hers and drew her down onto the couch next to him. He released her hand but remained close beside her.

"Dinner really was good," Maggie said, for little reason other than to fill the quiet. "Brandy enjoyed the candlelight. You should probably do that more often, to give her a treat." She was babbling and she knew it, but she was afraid of the silence.

"Brandy likes you," Ryan said softly.

Maggie started to tell him about what Brandy had said on the patio, then stopped. That moment seemed too precious to share yet.

"I really care about her, too," she said instead. Then, suddenly, she added, "Brandy never talks about her mother. Why is that?"

She sensed Ryan stiffening beside her and instantly regretted the question.

"I'm sorry. This isn't any of my business, I know. You don't have to answer that," she offered awkwardly.

At first she thought he really wasn't going to answer. He leaned against the back of the couch and stared away from Maggie, seeming to go somewhere else in his mind, far from the quiet living room.

"Brandy doesn't see her mother very much since she moved to Atlanta," Ryan said finally, still not looking at Maggie as he spoke. He felt the prickle of pain deep in his stomach that the thought of Delia always carried with it, even after three years. The broken dreams, for himself and for his daughter, remained like a bruise of sadness. The wound had stopped bleeding a long time ago, but the soreness persisted. "She's a corporate attorney with a large law firm there. She's good at what she does, I'm sure."

He turned to Maggie.

"She pops down here out of the blue every once in a while when she feels like it," he continued, and Maggie could feel the anger beneath his words. "She's a 'busy person,' she keeps telling me."

"How did you two meet?" Maggie found herself asking, pulled by the hurt she heard in his words and eager to know more about the complicated man beside her. She was afraid to lose the honesty and openness of the moment. She didn't want him to turn inside himself, the way she had seen him do so often, before she could learn more.

"We met in high school, in Columbia. That's where I'm from. My parents still live there," Ryan explained. "We were friends and then we started dating. Things just went on from there. We went to college together. We were always together. Her parents were friends with my parents, we had the same friends, et cetera, et cetera.

"We should have just left it at friends way back in the beginning, I guess," he said thoughtfully. "Looking back, I never really felt that romantic about her. Everything just seemed to snowball until our families and our friends expected us to marry. And Delia expected us to marry. That's her name—Delia," he said. "Of course I loved her. Just not in the right way. I think it was the same with her. I think she had this romantic dream about what our life would be like, and reality didn't turn out that way."

He fell silent.

"Is that why she left?" Maggie prodded gently, not yet ready for him to stop his story. It told her so much, this tale of young idealism. She wished she could have met the Ryan that existed then, before he'd built the shield that protected him now. "Was reality that painful for her?" Maggie prompted.

"I don't know," he answered slowly, shaking his head. "I think she felt something wasn't right, but we were both trying. Right after we married, we moved to Charleston for my job at the high school. We weren't planning to start a family right away. Delia had just started law school when she became pregnant. She was . . . upset. She wasn't ready for a baby."

Maggie fought the urge to reach out and touch him, to squeeze his hand. The pain behind the memories was palpable in the sudden silence of the living room.

Ryan's mouth set in a tight line. "We hired a sitter for Brandy right after she was born, and everything seemed fine at first," he continued. "Hectic—but fine."

He stopped and looked away from Maggie.

"Delia was wrapped up in her studies, and I was busy with my job and caring for Brandy during the evenings and weekends. We were living separate lives—and neither one of us did anything to change it. I have myself to blame for that as much as Delia. I don't know why I was so surprised when it happened. But I was."

"When what happened?" Maggie asked.

Ryan looked up at her. "When she left," he said quietly. "It was the day of her last exam. She came home and announced that she had an offer from a prestigious firm in Atlanta, and that was that."

"What about Brandy?" Maggie asked, shocked.

"You think I didn't ask that?" Ryan replied stiffly. "Delia said she was going to be putting in eighty-hour work weeks and that Brandy would be better off with me, since I could be with her more. She gave me full custody, as long as she could have visitation. The problem is, she doesn't visit much. She makes promises she doesn't keep—and Brandy is the one who ends up hurt." The bitterness in his voice seared Maggie.

"How old was Brandy?" she asked, an empathic hurt for the little girl growing inside her along with an understanding of Ryan's protectiveness. It was no wonder that he sheltered Brandy so cautiously, Maggie realized.

"She was only three," he said. "She doesn't really remember when her mother used to live with us. But she remembers her mother leaving—and she misses her."

Maggie frowned. "Does she talk about her mother a lot?"

"No." Ryan shook his head gloomily. "That would be better." He met Maggie's gaze squarely. "She has nightmares. She's afraid I'll leave her someday, too."

"Oh, no." Maggie stared at him. She recalled the day Brandy had found Maggie's packed suitcase in the bedroom. She also remembered how angry Ryan had seemed. "That's why she became so upset that time she saw my bag," Maggie said quickly. "And that's why you—"

Ryan grimaced. "Yes," he said, nodding.

"I'm sorry. If I'd known—"

"You couldn't have," Ryan said.

"Does she have these nightmares very often?"

"Not as much as she used to," Ryan told her. "I think they'll disappear completely, with time. She's only had the nightmare once since she began seeing you."

Maggie waited.

"It happened the night after she asked you to make her costume for the play," Ryan explained.

"She was upset because the other children had their mothers to make their costumes," Maggie guessed.

"You're helping her," Ryan said, his voice low but firm. His gaze warmed Maggie with its steady intensity. "She needs the kind of attention you give her. To her, her mother is just a woman who visits occasionally and sends birthday and Christmas presents. She's not someone who's there when Brandy needs her."

"I'm sorry." Maggie gently touched Ryan's arm. "I can see how close you and Brandy are. You're very protective of her."

"Yes, I am," he said. "Maybe I'm too protective sometimes."

"I don't blame you," Maggie said. "Brandy is a precious little girl. I'd be protective of her, too."

Ryan's brow furrowed. Long, silent seconds passed. The question that had long been in his mind rose to the surface. "Why have you never married?"

There was too much honesty between them in that moment for Maggie to answer with anything but the truth. "I've never been in love," she said simply.

Ryan's blue eyes deepened and intensified. "Never?"

"I don't really date much."

"I find that amazing," he said softly. "You're a very beautiful woman." He reached out and lifted Maggie's chin until her face was inches from his. He moved his fingers up to her cheek in a caress that sent shivering waves through her head, pulsating down to the rest of her body in sensual anticipation. She could feel the blood coursing, pumping through her veins as she met his blue questioning eyes.

Ryan's lips were almost touching hers, and then they were. He kissed her, softly at first, hesitant, then more forcefully until she thought she was drowning. Her head was spinning and she lost herself, giving in freely to the tenderness of his assault.

She knew she wanted more.

Chapter Five

Gently Ryan traced his tongue over the delectable curve of Maggie's lips, pressing between them until she opened her mouth to him. He moved his tongue in a seductive waltz, touching the inside of her lips, then her teeth, drawing her tongue against his. She responded, joining with him, sending fiery shots of adrenaline into his system.

Drawing back, Ryan trailed a line of kisses along Maggie's jaw, tenderly caressing with his mouth where he'd yearned merely to touch her before. Kissing was better, so much better, he thought as he lowered his attentions to explore the hollow at the base of her throat.

She arched her neck, a low moan escaping her lips as he twirled his tongue inside the soft dip where her neck met her chest. With great restraint, Ryan moved upward again, leaving a path of heat along the long line of her creamy neck until he found her mouth again. This time she moved against him, entering between his lips forcefully, pressing him backward against the couch.

Ryan pulled her against him as he leaned back, his arms encircling her body. Beneath his hands, he felt the beguiling softness of her skin through the thin blouse she wore. His fingers fell lower. He found her blouse untucked in the frenzy of their passion, and he pressed his hand inside and up until he settled on the clasp of her bra.

Maggie felt Ryan's fingers at her back, and knew what he desired. She turned from his mouth to drop tiny kisses along his chin and jaw, shifting slightly to ease his search for her clasp. Until the moment he'd touched her and shown her the riotous, erotic demand of his caresses, she hadn't realized just how much she'd longed for them. Now that he was here, with her, his hands moving like silken heat over her skin, she knew his embrace met the need that had grown within her from the day she'd met him.

With his hand slowly twisting the clasp of Maggie's bra, Ryan froze. The image of his daughter sleeping down the hall forced its way into his consciousness, followed by the dawning realization of what was actually happening between himself and the woman who was his daughter's special friend.

Suddenly Maggie felt Ryan's hands drop from her back as he pressed her away from his chest, against the couch. Maggie breathed in several short gasps and stared up into Ryan's dark eyes shadowed in the golden lamplight, revealing nothing.

She could see him retreating from her.

Ryan said, "I'm sorry. I didn't mean for that to happen." He pulled away then, not only physically but emotionally as his eyes hooded over.

"It's all right," Maggie told him, confused by his reaction, longing to retrieve their moment of closeness. She wanted to reach for him, to take back the warmth that had been between them. Only seconds before, he'd been arousing her, teasing her to the verge of sensual delight. Now a mask of coldness covered him, blocking him from her.

"No. No, it's not. I didn't want that to happen. I'm sorry." Ryan shifted slightly so that he was no longer touching her.

The whirling feelings within her held Maggie still a moment longer, then she rose abruptly, unsure who she was most angry with—Ryan or herself.

How dare he say he didn't mean to kiss her, didn't want to kiss her! She had certainly not been the one to kiss him. Not at first, anyway.

She'd very nearly allowed him to make love to her! She'd been about to reach behind her back to unclasp her bra. Another moment, and his hands would have been on her breasts, and his lips—she didn't even want to think about where they would have been next. And she would have let him. She didn't have any doubts about that.

"Of course, you're right," Maggie told him in short, clipped syllables. "I don't know what could have possessed us. I'll just be going." She picked up her purse.

He made no move to stop her, and when she realized she was actually hoping that he would, she was even angrier with herself.

"I'm sorry," he repeated.

She only just stopped herself from slamming the door.

"Is that all? Just a kiss? You're this upset about a kiss?" Emma questioned Maggie the next day over lunch at a restaurant a few blocks from Maggie's office.

"It's not just that," Maggie countered. "I don't know. He was opening up to me and then, *boom*, down came the shutters."

Emma poked a piece of lettuce with her fork, then looked up at Maggie narrowly.

"You're in love with him," she stated.

Maggie laughed sharply. "Right," she said sarcastically.

"Mag, I'm telling you, I can see it. You're in love. You just don't want to admit it."

Maggie shook her head at her friend. "I'm not," she repeated. "You just have a one-track mind."

"And he's falling in love with you, too," Emma continued.

Maggie shook her head again. "Now I *know* you're completely over the edge," she replied.

"I want you to be happy, that's all," Emma insisted. "I'm just mad that I can't claim any responsibility for this. I wanted to be the one to introduce you to your future husband."

"Future husband?" Maggie cried. "Since when have I ever said I wanted to get married? And if I ever did decide to get married, it sure wouldn't be to Ryan Conner!"

Emma smiled.

"I do believe the lady doth protest too loudly," she quoted loosely, smiling with a self-satisfied air.

"Forget it," Maggie said firmly. "Listen, the real reason I invited you to lunch today was to tell you my big news. I've been so busy that I haven't seen you in ages and I've got lots more important stuff to tell you than that Brandy's father kissed me."

"More important than romance?" Emma teased. "I doubt it."

Maggie ignored the comment. "I'm sure I've mentioned the District Achiever Award to you before. It's the highest award the company gives its employees. Just one person is nominated for it out of the entire district. Mike told me he put my name up for it this year."

"You're kidding?"

"No. I was flabbergasted myself," Maggie said.

"Well, of course you deserve it," Emma told her. "I didn't mean I didn't think you should have it. You're the best. I think it's great. I'm proud of you."

"I don't know if it's a curse or a blessing," Maggie said, laughing. "I've been so nervous ever since he told me. I wish I didn't even know."

"You'll win," Emma assured her.

"Oh, it's not that, really," Maggie replied. "I just feel like I have to live up to being nominated for it."

"You know, Maggie, the only person who isn't sure of you is you," Emma told her gently. "You do everything you set out to do, perfectly. I know you. You're a shoo-in." She pushed her salad plate away and cast a naughty grin at Maggie. "I just wish you'd set about getting a husband with the same energy you give your work. You could have Ryan Conner at your feet!"

Maggie sighed. "You're incorrigible, Emma. I give up."

Later, when Maggie was back at her desk, Emma's words haunted her as she tried to concentrate on the month-end sales reports.

You could have Ryan Conner at your feet.

Maggie took a deep breath and shook her head. She had to stop thinking about the man.

"As if I would want him at my feet," she whispered defiantly to herself in the closed office. "He can just *kiss* my feet, that's what he can do."

Ryan squinted as he sat at his desk, staring out the wide windows looking out over the high school courtyard. Students slowly filed into the large classroom, milling sociably around their desks. The bell rang in shrill reminder that the last class of the week was about to begin, sending students scooting to their chairs.

Usually Ryan looked forward to Fridays, to the last class before heading home for the weekend. But today was different. Tonight was Brandy's school play.

He'd promised Brandy they'd pick up Maggie on the way. Maggie was going to make last minute adjustments on Brandy's costume and help her go over her lines one last time.

Maggie was all Ryan had been able to think of all day.

Ryan grimaced to himself. All day? More like all week.

Maggie and her fiery red curls. Maggie and her generous smile and soft curves. Maggie and her lips on his.

"Mr. Conner?"

Ryan turned from the window, focusing on the students staring up at him from their neat rows of desks. The soft sounds of muted giggles broke the silence.

"Are we having class today, Mr. Conner?" a student in the front row asked, a mischievous gleam in his amber eyes.

"Yes, Jeff, we are," Ryan said, rising to pace the room. He stopped in front of the window. Suddenly he didn't feel like lecturing about Hawthorne's *The Scarlet Letter.* He didn't feel like talking to the class about anything.

Ryan pursed his lips and turned to face the room. "Today I want you all to write an essay. In class," Ryan said, the words tumbling off his lips as soon as the idea formed in his mind.

"About what?" one of the students prompted.

"Write an essay about the first time you did something, a first that sticks in your mind and changed your life," Ryan suggested impulsively.

"Like what? You mean like a first kiss?" a girl in the back row asked.

The image of Maggie's flashing green eyes closing in passion brushed through Ryan's memory.

"Or the first time you fell in love?" another girl added.

Several boys snickered. Ryan frowned.

"Anything you like," Ryan told the class abruptly. "But it has to be finished in fifty minutes."

He sat down at his desk, intent on grading grammar quizzes from an earlier period. Instead, Maggie hung over his thoughts.

Maggie, spitting fire that first day in the community center. Maggie, shyly, gently, nursing him the day he was sick. Maggie, blushing as she grew aware that she'd accidentally crashed dinner at his house. Maggie, her skin glowing hot with desire as he'd kissed her, his fingers running over the gentle silhouette of her back.

Ryan looked up at the class, his gaze falling on the girl who'd suggested writing about the first time she'd fallen in love, and he wondered if that was what she was really writing about. The girl was so young, not more than sixteen. Yet she'd already experienced first love.

And Ryan was thirty, and only now—

Ryan swallowed tightly. Could it be that he was falling in love with Maggie Wells? She haunted him day and night.

He'd certainly never really been in love with Delia. Not in the sense of true, passionate love. And neither had Delia been in love with him. Perhaps, he thought with a painful sort of clarity, if they'd ever truly been in love with each other, things might have turned out differently.

Might. There was always risk.

Maggie was risk. A risk Ryan wasn't sure he was ready for.

And not at all sure he could resist.

Maggie lifted a slat of the white miniblinds covering her living room window and stared out at the road in front of her house. Ryan and Brandy were late. She wondered if they were coming.

What if Ryan didn't want her to see Brandy anymore? She'd talked to Brandy only once since the disastrous night she'd dined at the Conner house. Ryan himself had been short with her on the phone, speaking to her only long enough to discover who she was before summoning Brandy to talk to her. Brandy had been the one to suggest picking up Maggie on their way to the play.

Everything had happened so fast that fateful night she'd had dinner with Ryan. He'd been talking, opening up to her for the first time, then suddenly he'd kissed her. His ardent explorations of her mouth and neck had left her limp, and hungry for more. Then, just as quickly, he'd withdrawn.

The mere thought of facing him tonight filled Maggie with humiliation. There was no pretending she hadn't responded—and how!—to his overtures that night. She hadn't been the one to pull back, either.

What must he think of her! Maggie let the slat drop from her finger.

Ryan could easily think she was so free with any man who came on to her. The truth was, Maggie couldn't remember the last time she'd even had a *date,* much less a kiss. She hadn't had anything remotely resembling a romantic evening with any man since she'd met Ryan, or for many months prior to their first encounter.

And she'd never been kissed the way Ryan had kissed her. She'd never felt the scorch of electricity that had thrummed through her veins at his touch, or the melting warmth that had settled over her heart. Nor had any man's kiss before induced such a complete loss of sensible thought.

Maggie's lips parted softly as she reflected on that night and on her reaction to Ryan's kisses. She reached up and pressed her fingertips to her lips, as if feeling again the brush of his mouth against hers.

Was this what love felt like? she wondered.

The low hum of a car engine sounded outside. Maggie peered through the slats of her miniblinds again and saw Brandy jumping out of the car and running up to the house. Maggie met her at the door.

"Are you ready?" Brandy asked. "Sorry we're late. I couldn't find my white shoes. Then I found them under my bed." She laughed, glancing down at her shiny white patent-leather Mary Janes.

"Well, I'm so glad you found them," Maggie said, taking Brandy's hand and hurrying along with the energetically skipping girl. To Maggie's chagrin, Brandy hopped into the back seat, leaving the front seat to Maggie.

Sliding in beside Ryan, Maggie smiled tightly, then stared straight ahead. The thought of meeting Ryan's eyes left her feeling mortified. The memory of their kiss loomed between them.

"I apologize for making you wait on us," Ryan said stiffly.

"No problem." Maggie continued staring at the road as Ryan pulled out into the street and headed toward Brandy's elementary school.

The tense silence between them would have been too thick to cut with a chain saw if Brandy hadn't been there to fill it. The little girl chattered without stopping. Maggie turned in her seat to face Brandy, nodding as Brandy carefully rehearsed her lines and giggled with excitement over the evening to come.

Her costume lay stored in a large paper grocery sack beside her, ready to be put on when they arrived at the school. Brandy leaned down and poked her hand into the bag, eagerly fingering the material.

"I'm going to have the neatest costume, don't you think, Maggie?" Brandy asked, her blue eyes glowing bright.

"Absolutely," Maggie assured her. "You're the prettiest spring flower I've ever seen."

Brandy smiled happily. Maggie remembered how the little girl had worried about not having a mother to make her costume. She recalled, too, the nightmares Ryan had said Brandy sometimes experienced.

Maggie shot a sidelong glance at Ryan, her brow furrowing as she wondered if Brandy had woken with any nightmares lately. Ryan turned and met her gaze. Maggie lowered her lids sharply, avoiding his eyes.

A moment later they arrived at the school parking lot. Ryan parked and Brandy tumbled out, holding her bag proudly in front of her. The little girl skipped ahead toward the door, disappearing inside the building and leaving Maggie walking uneasily with Ryan.

They reached the entry at the same time, their hands brushing against one another as they both moved to open the door. Maggie stepped back quickly, her fingers quivering with the electricity of Ryan's touch.

They both froze, their eyes meeting for several awkward seconds.

"Excuse me," Maggie said nervously.

Ryan stared at her, his expression enigmatic.

"You don't mind if I hold the door for you, do you?" he asked.

Maggie tried to smile. Or at least she did her best facsimile of one.

"Of course not."

Ryan pulled the door open and Maggie moved through the entry, taking care not to brush against him. But as she passed him, she couldn't help but breathe in the intoxicating scent of his musky after-shave. Every fiber of her ached with awareness of the crisp slacks covering his long legs, the soft cotton of his pressed shirt over wide shoulders and the searching intensity of his cobalt blue eyes.

Maggie gazed down the hallway, desperately needing some sign of Ryan's daughter. Brandy popped out into the hall from a side door that Maggie soon learned led to the back of the auditorium stage.

"Come on, Maggie, Daddy," Brandy called, waving to them. "I want to put my costume on."

Relief washed over Maggie. She hurried to Brandy, moving ahead of Ryan down the hall.

Half an hour later, with the flower costume shifted and smoothed into perfection over Brandy's small frame, and her lines rehearsed a final time, there was nothing left but for Ryan and Maggie to sit down in the auditorium.

They found seats in the front row in chairs so tightly packed together, there was no way to avoid their shoulders rubbing. Crossing her arms protectively over her chest, Maggie tried to make herself small. Irritation swelled within her that close proximity to Brandy's father could have such a disabling effect on her senses, especially after the fiasco of the weekend before.

She would have thought, she chastised herself, that these feelings would have diminished after Ryan's cool dismissal following their kiss. Instead, her flesh burned at the memory, her stomach knotted, her mind leapt about in confusion.

"Maggie?"

She jumped at the sound of her name.

"I'm sorry. I didn't mean to startle you," Ryan said, frowning. She'd seemed jumpy from the moment she'd gotten into his car. And he knew why. The kiss hung between them, leaving a haunting tension that was eating up his insides.

His daughter hadn't noticed the strain between them yet, but she would. He knew she would. Brandy could often be eerily sensitive to her father's feelings toward people. She'd known in the beginning that he was uncomfortable around Maggie. If he and Maggie became distant with each other again, Brandy would eventually notice.

Brandy had been so happy lately. She'd experienced only the one nightmare since Maggie had come into her life.

He couldn't risk allowing his relationship with Maggie to deteriorate to the point that Brandy noticed, Ryan told himself. He tried to ignore the tiny notion edging into the corner of his thoughts that it wasn't only because of his daughter that he wanted to ease the tension between himself and Maggie.

Ryan stared at Maggie beside him, his eyes soaking in her flame-colored hair and vulnerable green eyes. She looked as if she were waiting for him to pounce on her.

Parents and siblings noisily filled the auditorium around them. Ryan leaned close to Maggie.

"We need to talk," he said, his voice low.

Her gaze flashed up to his, questioning.

"About what?" she asked. But Ryan could see the embarrassment that pinkened her cheeks, and he knew she understood what he meant.

"About the other night," Ryan said.

"I fail to see why," Maggie replied tersely, turning to stare at the closed curtains onstage.

"Because Brandy's going to notice soon if we keep acting like this," Ryan said, his breath warm on Maggie's ear.

She turned and met his gaze. In his eyes, she detected a softening, perhaps even regret. Maggie lowered her eyes again, chewing on her bottom lip.

"I didn't mean to hurt your feelings," Ryan said.

Maggie's gaze flicked up to his sharply, anger fingering through her veins. He was apologizing for kissing her. Again.

"I'd hardly say my feelings were hurt," she told him, biting the words off in a chilly fashion. "Don't overestimate yourself. Or your kisses."

A grin curved the corners of Ryan's lips upward, surprising Maggie.

"Thank you," Ryan said softly. "I needed someone to put me back in my place. Consider me and my ego appropriately deflated."

Maggie stared at him a few seconds, then suddenly she felt nervous laughter rising. Ryan laughed with her. After a moment they stopped, still gazing at each other curiously.

"Friends again?" Ryan asked.

Maggie hesitated.

"Okay," she said, a sinking disappointment oozing up in her chest. *Friends,* he'd said.

Friends didn't kiss the way they'd kissed, she thought, her eyes moving almost of their own volition to his wide, generous mouth.

"For Brandy's sake," Ryan added.

"Of course," Maggie agreed.

The lights dimmed as the curtain rose and a hush grew over the auditorium. In moments, the school play began, telling the story of how spring brought the earth to life.

Maggie concentrated on watching the children perform, her eyes quickly seeking out Brandy. Her heart gladdened as she noticed with pride that Brandy did, indeed, have the "neatest" costume.

A soft touch on the back of her hand drew her attention away from the stage. She glanced down and saw Ryan's large hand covering hers. When she looked up, her eyes met his in the low light.

"Thanks," he mouthed.

Maggie smiled at him shakily. A few seconds later, Ryan moved his hand away. The lingering sensation of his touch remained on her skin, heating through her like a flash fire.

She knew they could never be friends.

Ryan swore softly as the sheaf of essays he'd been grading whooshed onto the floor around him. He hadn't been able to concentrate all morning. He kept thinking about Brandy and Maggie.

Actually, he corrected himself, it was Maggie he couldn't stop thinking about.

Maggie and Brandy were spending the day hosting a doll tea party on Maggie's lawn. The vision of Maggie in her low scooped-neck sundress, baring her silken shoulders and slender arms, persisted in Ryan's thoughts. His attention continually wavered from the student essays he was attempting to grade.

All he could think of was Maggie in her sunshine yellow dress, playing tea party with his daughter in the fresh spring breeze. The two of them were probably having a wonderful time right now, he thought gloomily.

Ryan sighed and leaned down to gather up the scattering of essays from his living room floor. Pen poised, he stared down at the papers. Empty silence closed in around him.

"Damn," he whispered, cocking his head backward and closing his eyes.

Maggie's emerald depths seared into his mind's eye.

Ryan opened his eyes and stood up, tossing the papers onto the couch. He grabbed his car keys up from the kitchen counter and slammed the front door behind him.

Chapter Six

Ryan brought his blue sedan to a slow halt in front of Maggie's house. Withdrawing the keys from the ignition, he fingered them in his palm as he stared out through the side car window at her house.

The front lawn was empty, so he assumed Maggie and Brandy must be around the back. He could still leave, he realized, and Maggie would never know he'd come.

He rested one forearm over the curve of the steering wheel and gazed with unseeing eyes out at the quiet residential street. Maggie was Brandy's special person, he chastised himself. He had no right to have these feelings for her.

And, on top of everything, Maggie was a dedicated businesswoman. Not that Ryan begrudged her a successful career, but he'd made a promise to himself when Delia left. He'd sworn never to allow a woman that close to him again who couldn't create a reasonable balance between her work and her personal life.

Maggie does have a balanced life, he told himself. She'd proven she could make time in her schedule for Brandy. If only Delia had given Brandy one-tenth of the attention that Maggie was giving her....

But would Maggie have time for both the father and the daughter? he worried. She never made a big deal of it, but he knew from little things she said, and from comments Brandy let drop, that Maggie often worked on the weekends and at night. Her position was demanding, and extra hours were required.

Maggie, he admitted to himself grimly, was a bright woman with a limitless future. So much like Delia. And yet so different.

Confused feelings mixed with a deep-seated fear inside Ryan. Keys clenched firmly in his fist, he opened the car door and stepped out. Frustration settled over him. There was no point in going back home. He'd never get those essays graded. He had to see Maggie, as if by simply seeing her he could somehow put all the questions in his heart to rest.

Ryan walked around the side of Maggie's home and slid quietly through the wooden back gate. Maggie, her legs tucked beneath her sun-bright cotton dress, was leaning forward to pour tea from a small white teapot into Brandy's china cup. She pretended to pour servings into cups that rested in front of Brandy's doll Penny and another doll.

Watching quietly, Ryan smiled as his daughter giggled at Maggie's cat lapping tea out of a white china saucer. A quilt of small, colorful rectangles lay beneath them, protecting their small tea party from grass and insects. The late-morning April sun shot speckled rays through the branches of the overhanging leafy oak tree, scattering a muted glow that caught at the fiery highlights of Maggie's hair. A light spring breeze strewed the sweet scent of azalea blossoms through the air.

Maggie leaned back as Ryan watched from the shadows of a pine tree near the gate. She repositioned herself, stretching out her long bare legs over the quilt. The soft curve of her calves drew his eyes. His gaze lingered over her legs, and he wondered what it might be like to touch her there, to run his fingers along the firm line of her calves to her thighs, and higher. His attention moved upward, to the slender tuck of her waist and the sensual bloom of her breasts. The dip of cleavage visible above the low neckline of her sundress tugged at his senses, leaving his mouth dry and his heart lurching.

His slow study moved upward and he met Maggie's curious eyes. She stared back at him in silence.

Maggie's stomach flipped. She lowered her lids shyly, but then, against her better judgment, glanced up again at Ryan. She wondered how long he'd been watching them. The intensity of his gaze told her he wasn't thinking of little girls and tea parties.

The erotic warmth in his darkened depths sent heated tingles shooting through her veins. He made her feel as if he were touching her already, his hands wandering over her skin, lighting flames of longing everywhere they passed.

"Maggie?" Brandy asked, her voice filled with confusion at Maggie's extended silence. The little girl turned around and spotted her father by the gate.

"Daddy! Come have tea with us," Brandy called. "Can I go get an extra cup, Maggie?" She turned to Maggie with pleading eyes. Maggie nodded, and Brandy ran toward the kitchen screen door.

Ryan strode leisurely across the crisp spring grass, his long legs encased in close-fitting blue jeans. Maggie brushed her tongue softly over her lips in a nervous gesture as she watched. Her mouth grew more dry and cottony the closer Ryan approached.

"Hi." Maggie waved her hand over the quilt. "Have a seat."

Ryan sat down so near, she felt the electricity jumping between them.

"Why are you here?" The words had tumbled from her thoughts to her mouth so quickly she hadn't had time to stop them. Maggie waited, her breath held tight in her chest.

A smile spread over Ryan's lips, reaching his eyes slowly. He stretched his long legs out in front of him before he spoke, leaning back with his weight resting on his hands.

"I couldn't concentrate on grading papers," he said at last, his expression sobering. The soft twittering of birds in the tree above them filled the brief silence before he added, "All I could think about was you."

"Me?" Maggie repeated, her lips parting in surprise. He'd been thinking about her? Excitement and fear wrestled inside her heart. Excitement that Ryan might care for her. Fear that her own feelings were making her jump to conclusions.

"Yes, you," he told her. She saw that he was laughing, and embarrassment burned over her.

"You mean, about us being friends again?" Maggie asked, falling back to safer ground.

Ryan lifted his brows in a skeptical fashion.

"Is that what you really want?" he asked, his voice low, his eyes tight on hers. "To be friends?"

"I—that's what we decided." Maggie swallowed thickly. "Isn't that what you want?"

Ryan reached over to take one of Maggie's hands into his own. He rubbed the back of her hand with his tapered fingers. The movement brought shivering delight spiraling up Maggie's arm. Ryan turned Maggie's hand over, one finger trailing sensually along the sensitive inner flesh of her palm.

He raised his gaze to meet Maggie's, his eyes dark with uncloaked desire. They stared at each other for silent seconds.

"I want—" Ryan began.

"Daddy, I have your cup," Brandy called, skipping toward them across the grass. Ryan dropped Maggie's hand, leaving her skin cold and bereft.

Brandy plopped down beside her father. Maggie dutifully filled Ryan's cup with lukewarm tea, willing her hand not to tremble—and failing.

Romeo mewed as he looked up from his now-dry saucer.

"No more for you, Romeo," Brandy cried, shaking her short finger at the white cat. "You're a pig. See, Penny and Sarah haven't even finished their first cup and you've had two saucers," she told the cat, pointing at the two dolls propped against the trunk of the oak. Brandy smiled at her father. "Maggie's cat really does drink tea, Daddy," she said gaily.

Maggie pushed Romeo back as he approached the plate of home-baked oatmeal cookies that she and Brandy had prepared that morning. Brandy chatted and Ryan agreeably consumed several cookies at his young daughter's request.

"I think Penny and Sarah have had enough tea," Brandy said at last. "Can I take a cookie to Mrs. Newley?" she asked. Maggie's neighbor, Mrs. Newley, had a collie with young pups and Brandy loved to visit the elderly widow and her puppies whenever she was at Maggie's house.

"Sure," Maggie said. She held the cookie plate out to Brandy, who snatched up a big round cookie and ran across the grass to the next house. Maggie busied herself by nervously picking up their tea things. She still felt a niggling remnant of discomfort around Ryan. Their relationship remained unclear. She didn't know where they stood with each other, and part of her was afraid to find out.

She gathered up their tea dishes. Scooping up as much as she could carry, she headed toward the house, studiously avoiding Ryan's eyes.

Nervousness threaded through her, and she knew he was watching her. When she was half-way to the kitchen door, the cookie plate teetered and fell from her full arms. Romeo hesitantly moved in on the cookies that lay scattered on the shadowed grass.

"Oh, go ahead now, you beast," Maggie said in frustration.

She looked up and found Ryan beside her, reaching for and relieving her of most of what she carried. His arms brushed against her chest, sending shock waves to her marrow.

"Let me help you," he said and, without waiting, walked ahead of her toward the house. Maggie stared after him, struggling to steady her reaction to his touch. After taking a deep breath, she followed Ryan into her clean blue-and-white kitchen and watched him set the tea dishes down on the white tiled counter.

"Thank you," she said shyly. She felt awkward and happy at the same time. The conversation they'd begun beneath the oak hung heavy between them in the silence of her kitchen.

Ryan walked past Maggie, so close she could smell his musky cologne. Without waiting for an invitation, he settled himself on her couch. She joined him in the living room, sitting down in an easy chair.

"This is very nice," he said, looking about the room.

He was uncomfortable, Maggie thought. She watched him curiously, finding his obvious unease with the situation endearing.

"I guess Brandy will be back any minute," Maggie said into the void of conversation. She wanted to say something, *anything,* to keep him from getting up and leaving. She'd dreamed of their being alone together again, and now that they were she couldn't think of a word to say.

Ryan rose suddenly and walked across the room to a bookshelf that spanned one wall. He casually strummed his fingertips along the edges of the books.

"Hemingway, Scott, Zola, Shakespeare," he read. "And a little Stephen King, as well. Such diverse tastes you have."

Maggie laughed with him.

"Those are mostly from college," she told him. "Not the Stephen King, of course," she said with a mischievous twinkle.

"I like horror novels myself," he said. "A little scare is good now and then." He looked at Maggie. "If you have nothing else to do in bed, of course."

"Of course," Maggie repeated, bewildered by the strange conversation he was leading her into.

Hot and cold, hot and cold, she thought. He was obviously hot right now.

Ryan watched the play of thoughts and feelings flitting across Maggie's face, wondering what she was thinking. His own thoughts strayed to his last comment about bed. The vision of Maggie, her hair splayed out on a pillowcase, morning sunlight streaming over her auburn locks, sent a quiver of yearning to the pit of his stomach.

The stunned look in Maggie's eyes at his suggestive words touched off a chord of softness within Ryan. Successful as she was in business, an air of innocence weaved around her, beguiling him.

"So we do have something in common then, don't we?" Ryan moved toward her until he almost stood over her. Maggie had to crane her head up to look at him. "Books, I mean."

"You thought we didn't?" she questioned.

He smiled and knelt beside her.

He's at my feet, Maggie thought suddenly, recalling her friend's admonition that she could have Ryan at her feet if only she tried. *Wait till I tell Emma.*

"A new production of *The Taming of the Shrew* just opened in one of the little theaters downtown. It's a modernized send-up, but I hear it's very good," Ryan said in a low voice beside her. His eyes reached out to hers and didn't waver as he continued, "Would you go with me to see it next Saturday?"

Maggie felt her heart lose a beat, and the thought flashed through her mind that she was glad she was sitting down.

"You mean, you and me? Without Brandy?" she asked. Whatever happened to mere friendship? she thought quickly.

He smiled again.

"Brandy has a sleepover at a friend's house that night." He reached out and took Maggie's hand into his again. "Let me be perfectly clear." His eyes twinkled. "I'm asking you out on a date."

"A date," Maggie repeated, rolling the word off her tongue slowly. "You mean, as friends?"

"I mean a date," he said, his gaze warm. "A friendly kind of date."

"I guess that's the best kind," she said, smiling.

"I think so," he agreed. "So you'll come with me?"

Maggie grinned wider. "I'd love to."

The sound of the kitchen screen door slamming shut broke the moment. Brandy skipped into the living room.

"Daddy! Daddy! Mrs. Newley says the puppies are old enough now to be adopted," Brandy announced, breathing heavily from her run across the grass between the two houses. "Can I have one? Please!"

A negative response came automatically to Ryan's mind, but before he could voice it, he glanced at Maggie. She was gazing at Brandy, smiling at the little girl's excitement. Maggie turned and grinned at

Ryan. He found his resistance to the dog melting under her expectant expression. He sighed.

"Okay," he told his daughter.

Brandy squealed and ran back out of the house, heading for Mrs. Newley's. Ryan shook his head.

"What?" Maggie asked.

"I seem to be doing a lot of things lately that I never thought I'd do," Ryan said wryly.

"Good," she said.

Back at home, dog and all, Ryan sat alone in a lawn chair watching his daughter romp with her new canine friend. He'd made two commitments he hadn't intended to make when the day started.

Both commitments had been sparked by Maggie's emerald eyes and sweet smile.

He hadn't meant to ask her to go to the play with him. He'd just intended to stop by. He'd just wanted to see her. The memory of Maggie sitting in the sunshine and shadows, sipping tea between those full pink lips, had stayed with him throughout the day after he and Brandy had returned home.

Looking back, he admitted to himself that he'd made up his mind to ask Maggie to spend time alone with him as soon as he'd set eyes on her under the oak tree. The vision she'd presented as she sat on the quilt—the light breeze playing delicately over shoulders bared by her sleeveless sundress—had broken his resistance. He'd known the truth then of why he'd gone to her house. He'd yearned to be near her, to touch her, to breathe in her subtle summer peach scent.

He couldn't pretend that she was only a friend. Not anymore.

Maggie and Ryan emerged from the little theater onto the cobblestoned Charleston street, laughing as they agreed on the production's humor and ingenuity. As they walked in and out of the glow of the old street lamps, Ryan took Maggie's hand and held it snug in his own. The touch was firm and proprietary, and Maggie's heart sang.

Once back in Ryan's sedan, they drove slowly through the streets of the Battery, the preserved pre-Civil War section of the city. It was a part of the city that always enchanted Maggie with its white-columned homes, cobblestoned streets and romantic, bittersweet past. But this night she found herself drawn to watch Ryan's profile rather than the antebellum architecture.

Ryan left the Battery and took a street that paralleled the ocean, then pulled over to the side of the road.

"Can I interest you in a moonlit stroll along the beach?" he inquired.

"I think you could," Maggie agreed with a smile.

She waited while Ryan walked around to open her door and take her hand as she rose from the car. Keeping her hand close in his, Ryan led her down a sidewalk beside the beach.

"Wait a minute," Maggie said, pulling her hand away. She leaned down and slipped her black pumps from her feet. Her toes, free of hosiery in the warm Southern evening, squished comfortably into the moist sand as she abandoned the cement walk.

"This feels great," she said, laughing up at Ryan. "You do it, too."

She could see him almost say no, then, reluctantly, he pulled off his leather dress shoes, revealing thin dark socks. With a rueful grin, he quickly whipped the socks from his feet.

"Catch me," Maggie challenged him. Dropping her shoes behind her, she ran toward the water, her heart racing with her feet. Seconds before she reached the glimmering shore Ryan grabbed her from behind, whipped her around to face him and tugged her close against his chest. She could feel his heart beating through his crisp white shirt.

"Did I tell you I ran track in college?" he whispered against her cheek.

Skin flushed, Maggie smiled into his eyes, only inches from hers.

"I'm so impressed," she teased. "Tell me more."

"What if I show you instead?" He burned a pattern across her cheek with his lips before moving to her mouth and kissing her, invading with his tongue. Maggie opened her lips to him, eagerly inviting him in, reveling in the hot passion of his seduction. Her eyes closed as her arms moved up his firm torso until her hands met behind his neck.

He whispered her name in a husky voice as he pulled away from her lips, nearly overwhelmed by the strength of her response. He lowered his passion to her neck, paving a track of fire down the sensitive column of her throat. Tenderly his heated attentions trailed farther and he pressed his lips along the soft rise of breastbone bared above her V-cut black dress. The feel of her heart thundering in her chest, the low moan sounding from her lips, awakened the floodgates of his long-repressed desire.

Maggie barely noticed the warmth of Ryan's fingers rubbing her back, so lost was she in the scorching motions of his tongue. She felt his movements increase in intensity as he discovered the dip and swell of her breasts, barely exposed along the upper edge of her dress. His hands moved around to her front, rising up her sides to caress the roundness of her breasts through the lightly clinging material that covered her.

Ryan groaned, suddenly abandoning his erotic explorations. Low against her stomach, Maggie felt a hardening, a quickening of masculine need.

Lips softly parted from the strength of his recent seduction, she stared at him. For a frightening moment, she saw him retreating, reminding her of the night he'd first kissed her and pulled back. She froze, waiting for him to speak.

Ryan inhaled deeply, the temptation bursting inside him giving clear evidence of the power of his inflamed need. If he didn't stop now, he wasn't sure he'd ever be able to. He'd almost waited too long to halt their lovemaking as it was. The longing to take her, right there on the deserted beach, burned hot from the core of his arousal.

"Maggie," he whispered. He brushed his hand along the satiny line of her jaw. "I can't take much more of this."

Relief washed over Maggie. He wasn't drawing away this time. Unexpected emotion flooded her heart, mixing with the desire. Emma was right, she knew suddenly. She loved him.

Ryan watched Maggie smile tenderly, her mouth still gently swollen from his sensual demands. Her green eyes darkened in sultry passion.

"I can't take much more of this, either," she told him, nearly setting off an explosion of carnal need in Ryan with the suggestively sexual curve of her lips.

Ryan forced himself to move his hand down from her cheek, along her side to link her fingers with his own. A curl of wonder thrilled through him when he felt the tremble of desire passing between them. The realization that she wanted him as much as he wanted her etched a tide of warmth through his entire body. With a gentle squeeze of her hand, he guided her along the water's edge at a leisurely pace in hopes of steadying his ardent yearnings.

Take it slow, he warned himself. *Don't rush.*

"There's something I've been wanting to tell you," he said as they walked.

Maggie watched the play of light and shadow across his face as he spoke, noting the intensity in his expression. Her veins still pulsated with the overwhelming power of the hunger they'd built for each other. A hunger she longed to fill with more of his steaming touch, more of his sensual lips, more of his heated urgency.

"I want to explain to you about the night you had dinner at my house," Ryan continued. "About what happened after we kissed."

He stopped walking and faced Maggie.

"I guess I feel sort of silly talking about it," he told her. "It's just that what I said came out the wrong way. I didn't mean that kissing you was something I didn't want to do. I did want to kiss you. I think I've wanted to kiss you since the first moment I laid eyes on you."

Maggie laughed. "You could have fooled me," she joked, the fiery memory of his most recent kiss still sizzling inside her.

Ryan smiled with her.

"It's Brandy," he explained.

"Brandy and I get along great," Maggie said.

"I know," he answered. "That's part of the problem. I felt like I'd be moving in on Brandy's turf if I pursued you romantically. I knew I was attracted to you, and I decided I absolutely wasn't going to do anything about it. Then that night you sat there beside me in the lamplight, so innocently sexy. I couldn't stop myself."

He put his arm around Maggie's shoulders.

"You were irresistible," he murmured, hugging her to his side, luxuriating in the feel of her form against him again. "I didn't mean to hurt you," he continued quietly. "After I kissed you, I tried to turn the clock back. But you can't go back."

"No," Maggie agreed. "And who'd want to?"

She leaned toward him impulsively and kissed his cheek. When she tried to pull away again, he tugged her to him, taking her mouth into his for a deep, tantalizing kiss before releasing her. She smiled again, breathless and flushed.

"Sit with me," he said suddenly.

"What?" Maggie exclaimed. "The man who didn't even want to take his shoes off now wants to actually sit on the beach in a suit?"

"That's right," he answered, and pulled her down with him, keeping her close to his side.

They leaned together in silence for several moments, listening to the soft lapping of the waves and watching the Atlantic tide roll. The moon splattered a changing trail of silver shimmers across the ocean.

This was wonderful, Maggie thought. She couldn't remember when she'd been this comfortable with a man. She'd never known such a fervent temptation for anyone, intermingled with a richly felt sense of caring and respect.

She'd never experienced the emotional and physical sensations that Ryan provoked. The glow in his gaze told her he felt the same.

"You amaze me," Ryan said.

Maggie turned to him and met his eyes.

"Do I?" she returned.

"You give so much of yourself to Brandy," he went on. "So much of your time and your energy. I know you're successful in your career and must have a lot of demands on your time, but you never make promises to Brandy that you can't keep."

"I wouldn't do that," Maggie told him seriously. "I won't let Brandy down."

"I know you won't," he said. "In the beginning, I was concerned about whether you would have time for Brandy. Because of that, I think you've been cautious about even talking about your work in front of me. But I want you to feel like you can talk to me about anything."

"I have been a bit afraid to talk about work with you," Maggie admitted. "It's a very important part of my life, of course. I enjoy my job, and I like to think I'm good at it," she said, a note of pride creeping into her voice. "I enjoy success at work. And I guess part of me needs it, as well," she added.

"What part of you is that?" he queried.

Maggie stared out at the ocean. There were parts of her heart she'd never shared with a man before. Letting Ryan inside, revealing the hurt she carried, frightened her.

"Maggie?"

Chapter Seven

"Hey, are you okay?" Ryan asked Maggie after several moments when she didn't answer.

"Oh, yes," Maggie answered huskily, turning to Ryan. "I was just thinking." Gazing up into his darkened eyes, she felt the encircling warmth of his concern. She remembered how he'd opened up to her about his past. She knew she had to be willing to be as open with him if they were ever to move forward in a relationship.

Maggie's nerves tightened, and she turned to stare out at the rolling rhythm of the ocean. Admitting her fears aloud didn't come easily to her. For too long, she'd suppressed them, kept them to herself.

No man had ever come as close to her heart as Ryan had. But releasing her defenses enough to let him inside—where he could see and understand the roots of her drive—sparked a new fear. Ryan had been terribly hurt in his life by a woman with a drive not so very different from Maggie's. She worried that confessing her deep-seated need for success could send Ryan into another retreat, just when they'd grown closer than ever.

"Maggie?"

She felt Ryan take her hand into his, pressing his fingers softly into her palm.

"You don't have to talk about this if you don't want to," Ryan told her, his voice low and gentle.

Maggie trailed a finger from her free hand slowly through the sand, considering his words. He wouldn't pressure her, she knew. But she knew as well that her fears would only grow if she kept them hidden.

They had to talk about her work and her past sometime. Maggie raised her head up, facing Ryan, studying his eyes.

"The part of me that needs success—and I mean success in a tangible form—is the part of me that's still nine years old and scared to death of the world." Maggie watched Ryan. He met her gaze quietly, his eyes questioning. She looked away, back at the Atlantic, and continued. "My need to be successful has a lot to do with my need to be self-sufficient—in control, I guess." She laughed shortly. "Or at least that's what a counselor in college told me once. I used to have anxiety attacks before exams and I went to see a counselor a few times."

She looked again at Ryan. His eyes on hers revealed little. Maggie took a deep breath and exhaled slowly.

"I just don't ever want to have happen to me what happened to my mom," she said at last.

"What happened to her?" Ryan asked. "I've never heard you mention your family." He heard the pain behind Maggie's words. Opening up this way clearly came hard for her, and he longed to pull her against him and kiss the hurt away. But he knew from his own life that denying pain could sometimes do the worst harm of all.

"I don't usually think, much less talk, about the past because it makes me sad," Maggie told him.

Ryan's blue eyes softened as she talked. The words came slowly, but Maggie felt the beginnings of release as she told Ryan the story of her parents, of her father's clothing business and eventual bankruptcy. The confusion and tears of those days rose up inside her, lodging thickly in her chest. She felt a tremble in her fingers, then Ryan's hand closed tighter around them, supporting her with his quiet strength.

"We lost everything in the end," she explained. "Even the house. I was only nine, so I don't really know what happened. I think my father just wasn't a very good businessman. He tried, but he just couldn't make a go of it.

"He had a heart attack the day before the bank took the house," Maggie said. She saw the question in Ryan's eyes, and continued before he could speak. "He died," she said simply. "All I remember of that time was just being confused. I was scared. I didn't understand what was going on.

"My mother was in a depression for a long time, although I didn't have the words to describe it back then," Maggie continued. "She didn't have any skills—she'd always depended on my father. We didn't have any close family. Not any that my mother would go to, anyway.'' Maggie bit pensively on her lower lip before adding, ''We spent the first month in a community shelter. We'd always had everything—a nice home, clothes. I had all the toys I could want. Then, suddenly, we had nothing.''

An old ache shot through her at the thought of the shelter, of the constant fear and bewilderment she'd felt as a child there. She remembered nights on the shelter's hard, narrow cot, her small body hugged tight against her mother's, panicked every moment that somehow her mother would be taken from her, too.

''Maggie,'' Ryan whispered softly, an answering hurt seeping over his own heart as he realized the desperate circumstances she'd experienced. It gave him a shock to think of Maggie dealing with such pain when she was not much older than Brandy.

''My mother, who'd never worked a day in her life, ended up working a lot of manual, tedious jobs,'' Maggie went on, her voice growing stronger as she pushed back the memories of terror from that first awful month. ''She took whatever she could get. I worked my way through college myself, and I tried to help her after I graduated. But by the time I could help her, she didn't really need it.''

''What do you mean?'' Ryan asked.

Maggie smiled wryly. ''It's kind of funny, in a way. It's the sort of thing that never happens, or at least that's what you'd think. My mother cleaned houses. She worked for years for one particular couple and then his wife died. About a year later he asked my mom out,'' Maggie explained. ''They got married, he retired and they live in Florida now in a condo on the beach. I go down and see my mom a couple of times a year. Philip—that's her husband—is a really nice man, and he treats my mother like a queen.

"He rescued her, in a way. She was really getting too old for the kind of work she was doing, and he's so wonderful to her. But I have to admit that it bothers me a little that she was so dependent on my father, and now she's the same way with Philip. Ever since I was a little girl I've been determined not to ever end up like my mother," she finished. "I can take care of myself. I *have* to take care of myself."

She felt cold in the silence that followed, then Ryan pressed his arm tighter against her side, twisting her toward him. He reached out with his other hand and tilted her face up to his, then leaned forward and lightly kissed her cheek.

"It's not always a terrible thing to depend on other people," he said, his words sounding like the most tender of caresses to Maggie's ear.

She leaned against him, and it occurred to her that allowing herself to become dependent, emotionally, at least, on this sensitive man would be very easy.

But would he always be there for her?

The question frightened her.

"Things are going well, then, I presume?" Mrs. Fletcher questioned, staring across Ryan's living room to Ryan and Maggie. They sat together on the couch, with Brandy sandwiched between them.

"Great," Ryan said, ignoring the uncomfortable twinge in his gut that Mrs. Fletcher's stern eye inspired. He'd thought scheduling the final check-in with the social worker was a waste of time to begin with, especially on a beautiful Saturday afternoon. As far as Ryan was concerned, the community center no longer had anything to do with Maggie's relationship with Brandy. "Things are great." He looked at Maggie warmly, his mind drifting to their evening out together.

The social worker's eyes narrowed, and Maggie shifted in her position on the couch. She could see Ryan was eager for the meeting to be concluded, and she suspected Mrs. Fletcher had noticed the same thing. After asking several more questions about Maggie and Brandy's activities, Mrs. Fletcher suggested in a pointed manner that Brandy might care to go outside and play with her dog for a few minutes while she talked with Ryan and Maggie. After the little girl cheerfully bounded out through the glass doors, Mrs. Fletcher turned her gaze on Ryan and Maggie. She sighed heavily.

"Is there a personal relationship between the two of you?" she asked them in a flat, no-nonsense voice.

Maggie looked at Ryan. She tried to keep a straight face, but couldn't stop her lips from curling upward.

"Yes," Ryan answered the social worker. "You're correct about that."

"I see," Mrs. Fletcher said.

"Is there some problem with that?" Maggie asked.

"I suppose not," Mrs. Fletcher said slowly, her voice implying that she really thought the opposite. "Of course, one has to be concerned that the child isn't left out now that you two have, well, found each other, so to speak. The purpose of this program is to provide a special relationship for the child, not the parent." Her steely-eyed glare settled accusingly on Maggie.

"I spend as much time with Brandy as I ever did," Maggie assured her. "More, actually." Now that her relationship with Ryan had graduated to another plane, she spent more time than ever at the Conner home. More time with Brandy, and more time with Ryan. The past few weeks had been wonderful.

Sometimes, she almost felt as if they were a *family.* It was an eerie, yet delightful, sensation. One she hadn't truly experienced since her father's death.

"That's all fine and good for now," Mrs. Fletcher went on, a note of warning creeping into her voice. "But what happens if the two of you come to. . . shall we say, a parting of the ways? You have to think about the impact on the child."

"I believe I'm more than capable of seeing to my own child's welfare," Ryan said stiffly. "I wouldn't allow my relationship with Maggie to interfere with Brandy's needs." He stifled another curl of trepidation. The fact that Mrs. Fletcher, a virtual stranger to his child, felt comfortable making judgments about his personal life irritated him.

The possibility that she might be striking too close to the nerve didn't bear thinking about.

Maggie shot a curious gaze at Ryan, surprised at his unexpectedly icy response to Mrs. Fletcher. Maggie couldn't remember seeing Ryan behave this coolly toward anyone since, well, since she'd first entered Brandy's life. He'd been so concerned then that she would allow her work to overshadow her obligations to Brandy.

But she and Ryan had grown past those early concerns that had kept them apart. Hadn't they?

"Brandy's needs come first with me—with both of us," Maggie told Mrs. Fletcher, trying to infuse confidence into her voice, but knowing she sounded as uneasy as she felt.

Later that afternoon, as Maggie sat in a lawn chair in the shade, watching Ryan putter in his garden, Mrs. Fletcher's words came back to her, haunting her. She couldn't even remember what they'd discussed during the rest of the meeting. What if they did have a "parting of the ways," as Mrs. Fletcher had put it?

Ryan's cool reaction to Mrs. Fletcher's probing still worried her.

Ryan put down his hoe and came toward her, sweat glistening on his tanned skin. He sat down in the chair beside her, bent toward her and kissed her cheek.

"Hey, beautiful," he said, then asked, "why so serious?"

"I was thinking about what Mrs. Fletcher said," Maggie replied. "About us, I mean."

"What's the problem?"

"That doesn't bother you?" she asked.

"Doesn't what bother me?"

"All that stuff she was saying about how we shouldn't be seeing each other because of Brandy."

"Don't borrow trouble, Maggie," he said lightly, frowning. Spotting his daughter heading their way, he mentally shook off the vague chord of apprehension Mrs. Fletcher's warnings had evoked. "Speaking of trouble," he muttered, smiling. Brandy ran toward them, her puppy, Goldie, fast on her heels. The little girl laughed as she reached her father and hid behind his chair.

"Down!" Maggie cried as the dog leapt against her leg.

Ryan pulled the puppy away from her.

"I still can't believe I let you talk me into allowing your neighbor to give Brandy this dog," he said to Maggie as the young collie jumped excitedly up at him and licked his face. Brandy giggled behind him, then leapt up and ran, her laughter floating on the wind as the dog chased her again.

"I must have taken leave of my senses," Ryan said, grinning at Maggie. "There's only one explanation."

"And what's that?" Maggie asked playfully, pushing back her fears. Her heart pounded as she looked up into Ryan's sparkling blue eyes.

"I'm crazy for you," Ryan replied.

"How come you just now told me this?"

Maggie stared at Ryan. She'd finally decided to tell him about the District Achiever nomination.

"I don't know," she said softly, unsure how to answer. Her gaze swayed over the shadowed living room of Ryan's house. After Ryan had finished his gardening chores, they'd eaten dinner, and Maggie had been firmly shooed from the kitchen when it was dishwashing time. Brandy was finally in bed, and Maggie and Ryan were enjoying their precious time alone together, snuggling on the couch, country-western music playing softly on the stereo.

"I'm not used to having someone to share these things with," Maggie said finally.

Ryan's arm around her shoulders drew her closer. "You have someone now."

Maggie chewed her bottom lip for a second, wanting to just revel in the closeness, yet knowing she had to say more. "I wasn't sure you really wanted to hear about my work," she admitted, and waited.

"Maggie, I want to be part of your life," Ryan said quickly. "I want you to share things with me." With his free arm, he moved to stroke her cheek with his long fingers. "I'm proud of you for this nomination."

A warm feeling trickled through Maggie. She snuggled deeper into the cradle of his shoulder.

"That means a lot to me," she said. And in Ryan's arms, in the nighttime quiet of his living room, she shared her dreams. She told him she was the youngest employee ever to be nominated for the award, how surprised she'd been when Mike Roberts had broken the news and how she was on tenterhooks as she waited for the awards ceremony.

Ryan listened, watching the shine in Maggie's eyes as she talked. She was in her element, confident and exhilarated.

When she finished, Ryan leaned forward to plant a heated kiss full on her lips. He drew back slightly. "I'm glad you're happy," he said huskily, his gaze locking with hers. "Thank you for including me."

He kissed her again, then his mouth lowered to her throat, then the hollow at the base of her neck. He swirled his tongue inside the tiny dip, sending shivers of enticing sensations bubbling through Maggie's blood.

"Daddy? I can't sleep." Brandy padded softly into the room.

Ryan drew back, his darkened gaze on Maggie showing his regret. She gave him a small, empathic smile, still feeling shivery and weak from his kisses.

Still wishing for more.

She knew he did, too, even though he stood up then. He could hardly tear his eyes off her to look at his daughter.

"Will you read me another story?" Brandy asked.

Ryan hesitated, but in the end, he said, "Okay, sweetie. Go on back to bed. I'll be right in."

Brandy padded away. Maggie stood and reached for her purse and car keys from a side table.

"I need to go home anyway," Maggie said, smiling ruefully at Ryan. "I still have my packing to do, and I need to work on my speech."

Maggie was speaking at an industry conference in Boston. The conference would last most of the week, and she had a flight scheduled for the next day. She'd already told both Ryan and Brandy about her plans, trying to be careful now to let the little girl know in advance of her trips.

Ryan touched his fingertips gently to Maggie's chin.

"We'll miss you," he said softly. He shook his head. "*I'll* miss you."

"I'll only be gone four days," she reminded him lightly.

"I have a teacher workday this Friday," he remembered. "Brandy will be spending the day with one of her little friends. Can you spare an hour for lunch? You can tell me about your trip."

Maggie nodded. "I'd love to."

Ryan made the plans quickly, naming a popular downtown restaurant near Maggie's office. "Friday at noon."

"I'll be there," Maggie promised.

Maggie jumped as the phone rang, interrupting her train of thought. She was attempting, for the umpteenth time Friday morning, to organize her notes from the Boston conference. Mike Roberts, at home recovering from a bout of appendicitis, called her every fifteen minutes with more questions, eager for details from the full report, which she'd promised to have on his desk Monday morning when he returned to work.

She grabbed the telephone receiver in annoyance, knocking to the floor the stack of the mail accumulated in her absence. As she put the receiver to her ear, her secretary knocked.

"Hang on, Mike," Maggie said into the receiver in distraction, then looked up at the secretary.

"Your eleven o'clock's here, Maggie," she said.

"Give me two minutes," Maggie told her. "Mike?"

"Maggie?"

The voice jolted her into awareness.

"Ryan! I'm sorry. I was expecting my boss. He's been calling me nonstop about the conference. It's a madhouse here today," Maggie explained. "I hate the first day back from a trip."

"How'd it go?"

"Oh, Ryan, the speech was great! I actually enjoyed delivering it," Maggie continued. "I thought I'd hate it, but I didn't. I mean, I've made presentations before, of course, but not to an audience this important. It was really fun. I'm still on a high from it," she confessed. "I guess you can probably tell."

"Oh, maybe a little," Ryan teased her.

Maggie was struck suddenly by the realization that it felt absolutely wonderful to have someone special, someone who cared, someone with whom she could share her excitement. The feeling rippled through her, new and delightful and warm.

A knock on the door told Maggie that her eleven o'clock was on his way in.

"Ryan? I've got to go. I have an appointment." Her secretary cracked the door and peeked in. "I'll talk to you later," Maggie promised. "Bye."

At two o'clock Maggie's secretary popped her head into the office and asked, "Do you want me to have some lunch delivered? A sandwich or anything?"

Maggie dropped her pen on her desk and her head shot up.

"Oh, no," she moaned. "Lunch." She put her head in her hands, her hair falling into her face. "How could I do this?"

"It's not too late to order out," her confused secretary offered.

"No, no, I don't want anything." Maggie waved her away. "Thanks, anyway," she added as an afterthought.

How could she? she berated herself. She hadn't even remembered their date when Ryan had called. What must he think?

Work, work, work. That was all she'd talked about. She'd been so full of herself, she thought. Then she'd brushed him off because she had had her appointment coming in.

She looked around for her phone book. She'd never called him at the high school before. Then she remembered suddenly that he had a teacher workday. Did that mean he was at the high school or at home?

Dialing his home number, she listened to the phone ring unanswered. She finally hung up and hurried to the outer office.

"Where's a phone book?" she demanded. Her secretary calmly handed her the thick book from atop her desk and watched as Maggie flipped through it.

"Can I help you with—" the secretary began, but Maggie ran back into her office with the book and shut the door behind her. She picked up her pen and punched in the number.

"I need to speak to a teacher—Ryan Conner," she requested in an assertive tone.

"Is this an emergency?" the voice at the other end of the line asked.

"Yes," Maggie answered. "No. I mean, it is to me, but I guess it isn't an official emergency."

"Who's calling?"

"Maggie Wells."

"I'll see if I can get him," the voice said.

Maggie waited. And waited.

"Mr. Conner has already left for the day," the voice finally told her.

Maggie sighed.

"Can I take a message?"

"No, just forget it," Maggie said, realizing he wouldn't get the message till Monday. She'd talk to him before then.

Okay, Maggie thought, forcing a slowing of her pulse, *it's just lunch. It's not the end of the world. Don't go crazy over this.*

But that was easier said than done as she tried to finish up the Boston report. She concentrated with difficulty the rest of the day, stopping twice to call Ryan. She never reached him, and it was six-thirty before she had the report tied up. That still left the onerous Friday duty of preparing the weekly report. Maggie finally shooed her weary secretary home, remaining alone to finish the paperwork.

She could barely hold her eyes open as she drove to her house through the dark, realizing with a twist of her stomach that she'd missed both lunch and dinner. Home at last, she stared at the kitchen tiredly, then decided food was more trouble than it was worth.

Trailing back to her bedroom, Romeo at her heels mewling anxiously for his dinner, Maggie thought about calling Ryan again. She flopped down onto her bed, her hair spilling out around her.

The truth was, she decided as she stared dully up at the ceiling, she was too exhausted to speak to her cat, much less another human.

She had a date to take Brandy to the children's theater the next morning. Tomorrow, she thought, sighing to herself. She could explain it all to Ryan then.

But would tomorrow be too late?

Maggie fed Romeo, because it was the only way to silence him. Then she stripped off her dress, hosiery and shoes, leaving them all in a heap on her bedroom floor, and fell onto the bed in her white lace bra and panties. She was just going to rest her eyes for a few minutes.

Then she would call Ryan.

Chapter Eight

"Daddy?"

Ryan stopped in the doorway of Brandy's room, turning at the soft sound of his daughter's voice. He saw her eyes, round in the dim light, staring up at him.

"You're supposed to be asleep," he said, walking back to sit on the bed beside her. He reached up and brushed his hand down her cheek tenderly, then kissed her nose. He'd expected her to fall asleep quickly after their busy afternoon. After Maggie hadn't shown up at the restaurant, he'd picked up Brandy and her friend and taken them to the park, the mall and then out for pizza.

He'd done anything he could think of to keep his thoughts away from Maggie, from the bitterness that had risen with haunting familiarity. All his efforts had failed miserably.

He knew he should brush off the entire episode. She'd stood him up accidentally. She'd been excited and busy with her work.

She'd simply forgotten.

"I was almost asleep," Brandy said, cutting into Ryan's thoughts. "Then I woke up again."

"Well, go back to sleep." Ryan forced himself to focus on his daughter. "You're not conning me into reading another chapter. I already read two. Go to sleep," he told her again gently, starting to rise.

"I was just thinking about Maggie," Brandy said.

Ryan sat down again and waited. He didn't really want to talk about Maggie right now.

"Maggie's really neat, don't you think?" Brandy asked.

Ryan nodded. "Sure," he said automatically.

"Do you think she'll always be my friend?"

"What makes you ask that?" Ryan said, stalling.

"One of the kids in my class told me she had a special grown-up friend from the community center last year, and that now she doesn't see her anymore. She said she didn't mind, but I could tell she did. I'd really mind if Maggie stopped being my friend." She tilted her head. "You'd mind, too, wouldn't you, Daddy?"

A tingle of trepidation brushed along Ryan's nerves.

"I want you to be happy," Ryan said, uncertain of how to reassure his daughter.

"I don't think Maggie will ever stop being my friend," Brandy said, brightening suddenly. "That's what I told Jenny at school. She's the one who told me her grown-up friend stopped coming to see her. She told me Maggie would stop coming to see me someday, too. I told her Maggie loves me and she's going to be my friend forever."

Ryan swallowed tightly.

"You need to close your eyes now and get some sleep," he said quietly. "You have to be ready early tomorrow. Maggie's taking you to the children's play, remember?"

"Okay." Brandy squeezed her eyes shut in overzealous obedience. Ryan kissed her again and left the room.

He slumped onto the couch in the living room. *The purpose of this program is to provide a special relationship for the child, not the parent,* Mrs. Fletcher had said. He could still remember the disapproving chill in the social worker's eyes as she'd spoken, and the apprehension he'd felt at the time.

And he recalled sitting at the restaurant, alone. An old ache fingered into his heart, remembered hurt throbbing in familiar places. He should have been able to let it go—it was just a lunch, after all. But he couldn't let it go. Instead, he felt this terrible, aching bitterness. A bitterness that he knew only too well.

He didn't like the feelings, or the person those feelings had made him become once.

It had taken him years to chip through the hardness his marriage had plastered over his heart. With only the smallest of incidents, Maggie had brought it all back.

How many nights had he waited for Delia when she'd promised to be home at a certain time to share dinner with him and spend the evening with Brandy? Instead, she would stay late at the library, studying. She would forget about her husband and child at home, so enthusiastically was she immersed in her studies.

She'd promise to do better. And then she wouldn't.

Eventually she'd stopped promising.

Their marriage had been over a long time before she left. The signs had all been there, if only he could have read them, Ryan thought with the sharp sight offered by time's passing.

Instead, he'd hung in, and he and Delia both had become people neither of them wanted to be. The bitterness had been nearly palpable between them during the divorce—so much disappointment and regret and blame. Delia's first few visits to Brandy had been disasters of barely concealed confrontation.

Could he risk repeating the same scenario? Brandy wanted Maggie to be her friend *forever.*

What right did he have to jeopardize Brandy's happiness? What would happen if he and Maggie went on, and their relationship ended badly? Brandy would be caught in the middle. Again.

He'd been fantasizing a future with Maggie all these weeks. Fooling himself that they could build a world together, one that would last a lifetime. One in which the pain of the past would never intrude.

In reality, all he'd really done was set them all up for a fall. A fall he'd taken once before, and had no intention of taking again.

Maggie braked in front of Ryan's house and stared through the trees to the house as if searching for some hint of the mood inside. The curtained windows looked blankly back at her.

She'd woken an hour earlier and realized that not only had she fallen asleep without calling Ryan last night, she'd also overslept this morning in her exhaustion. Looking at the clock by her bed, she knew she'd never make it in time for the children's theater. She almost called Ryan right then, but knowing he was probably already irritated with her, she had decided to dress quickly and drive over instead. She suspected that explaining would be awkward enough at this point without doing it over the phone.

She got out of the car, slammed the door shut and walked resolutely up to the house. Ringing the doorbell, she thought over what she'd say to Ryan, as she had done all the way there.

Ryan opened the door.

"Come in," he said, his voice telling her nothing.

Maybe he wasn't upset, after all, she thought. Maybe, in her mind, she had been making a mountain out of a molehill.

She brushed past him closely, the familiar electricity jittering through her as always when he was near. Once in the living room she turned to face him.

"Well, let me get this out of the way first thing," she said in a direct and practical tone. "I'm sorry about lunch yesterday. It was so hectic that I just forgot. I tried to call you later, but I couldn't get a hold of you. And even worse than all that, I was so tired from work that I fell asleep as soon as I got home, and then I overslept this morning and missed my date with Brandy. Was she awfully disappointed?"

"Yes, she was looking forward to it," Ryan replied. His voice was cool, almost impersonal. "When you didn't come and didn't call, she was upset."

"I'm sorry. I feel terrible, believe me," Maggie said. "I woke up a little while ago, and I thought it would be best if I just came right over."

She took a step toward Ryan and added huskily, "You understand, don't you?"

She raised her arm to touch his chest, but he withdrew a step. Maggie dropped her hand and searched his expression, hard and serious as he faced her.

"You're angry," she accused him, frustration welling up. "I know I made a mistake. I made a couple of mistakes. But these things happen, Ryan. I was busy yesterday, and I just forgot about lunch. And you know I would never purposely let Brandy down. Don't you ever make mistakes or miss appointments?"

"Yes," he said quietly. "I do. I make mistakes, too. And I think this is one of them. This isn't going to work. You can see that, too, I think."

"I don't even know what you're talking about," Maggie answered, irritation rising within her along with a tremble of fear.

"This isn't only about lunch, or about you missing your date with Brandy," Ryan said baldly. "It's about priorities. Ours are different. We can't keep on pretending that this isn't true."

"Our priorities aren't that different," Maggie cut in. "We both care about Brandy—"

"I know you care about Brandy," Ryan said. "You're a wonderful friend to her. And that's the way it should be. That's the kind of relationship that fits your life." His voice was even, emotionless. "Your career comes first with you. And there's nothing wrong with that—for you."

"I have room in my life and my heart for more than that, Ryan," Maggie told him softly, shaking her head. "My career is very important to me. You've known that from the start. But in the months since I've known Brandy—and you—I've changed. I want more."

"Really?" Ryan asked her, painful disbelief woven through his voice. "Come on, Maggie. What's changed? Think about it." His gaze bored into hers. "If work wasn't first with you, you'd already have a daughter of your own."

Maggie stared at him, frozen for a moment.

"That's not a fair comment, Ryan," she returned at last.

"I'm sorry. Maybe you're right about that, at least," he agreed in a softer voice. His expression gentled then, and something akin to regret sparked in his deep blue eyes. When he continued, his voice was lower. "But I think you're lying to yourself and to me if you try to convince us both that you really have time to be with a family," Ryan said. "It's not just missed lunches or outings. It's trips to Boston and Baltimore and everywhere else. That's your life, Maggie. And you like it that way. You chose it. But it doesn't fit with my life and it never will. This just made me realize it sooner instead of later.

"I'm not going to be able to accept your life-style, and I think we should just end this now," he continued. "There's no future to it. If we try to go on, there will be more missed dates and more trips and more arguments. That's just the way it is," he ended.

The depth of defeat in his voice shook Maggie. Her heart thumped in her chest, sudden fear shooting adrenaline through her veins.

Maggie lashed out at him. "You're a coward, Ryan Conner. And you're wrong. You were burned once so now you judge every other woman by Delia. Well, I've got a news flash for you. I'm not your ex-wife. Just because I missed one lunch date with you or one outing with Brandy doesn't mean that my career means more to me than people do. You're over-reacting."

"No," he replied quietly, shaking his head. He took her hand gently, and the sorrowful flatness in his eyes scared Maggie more than anything he'd said. "Maggie, I don't want to hurt you. I just want to stop this before it goes any further. You and Brandy come first. She loves you and I want you to keep on seeing her. I don't want us to keep going, to keep pretending, until we make such a mess of all this that it becomes difficult for you to continue to see Brandy. Let's end this now before it's too late."

Before it's too late? The words reverberated inside Maggie's head. *Like before she fell head over heels hopelessly in love with him?*

"Well, I'm glad this was such a casual thing for you," Maggie said, unable to restrain the bitterness in her voice. "But I think I'll find it a bit hard to be friends now. You can't go back, remember?"

Her voice shook slightly at the end as she recalled the night on the beach when Ryan had said those same words to her, and kissed her and held her close.

"You're using Brandy as a shield," Maggie added quietly, struggling to steady her voice. Emotion flowed close to the surface, nearly choking in her throat as she spoke. "You're not afraid I'll leave Brandy. You're afraid I'll leave you." She caught his gaze in hers, challenging him to deny it. And in that moment, she saw the truth in the numbed hurt flickering in his blue eyes.

Ryan averted his gaze from Maggie's, staring stonily out through the sliding glass doors. Outside, the morning beamed bright and clear, typical May in Charleston.

He couldn't stand to look at Maggie in that moment. He knew she was right.

Silence pressed down over the room, heavy in its aching fullness.

Yellow butterflies flitted across the spring grass outside. Ryan could hear Brandy laughing as she played with her puppy in the yard.

"I never wanted to hurt you, Maggie," he said finally, his voice close to a whisper.

"Ryan—" Maggie began in a raspy whisper. One tear, then another, escaped and trailed down her cheek. She inhaled a shaky breath, steeling herself to hold back the floodgates of emotion that threatened to roar open.

More silent seconds ticked by.

She wiped at her cheek, hiding her tears before Ryan could turn and see them. "Where's Brandy?" she asked quietly, the merest of trembles revealed in her voice. She had to change the subject. She was scared that if she didn't, she might start begging. She loved him that much, wanted him in her life that much. But she wouldn't—couldn't—beg him to be there. Not when he didn't want to be.

Ryan turned suddenly and faced her again, his eyes unreadable. Shielded.

"I want to apologize to her myself," Maggie said. "I'd like to take her back to my house for lunch, if you don't mind."

I have to get out of here, she thought. The burning sensation behind her eyes frightened her. She didn't want to let another tear fall, to show him how much he'd hurt her, to let him know she loved him.

"Maggie—" Ryan began, then stopped short. "I'll get Brandy," he said gruffly.

He went to the back door and called his daughter.

"Hi, Maggie," Brandy greeted a few moments later, panting, cheeks flushed.

Ryan shut the glass doors to the backyard behind her as she bounded into the living room. He stood near the door, waiting, withdrawn.

"I've been playing with Goldie," Brandy told Maggie. "I'm teaching her tricks. She fetches really good now. But I can't get her to stop jumping on me." She wrinkled her forehead. "How come you didn't come to take me to the show this morning? I thought we were going to go."

"I'm sorry, Brandy," Maggie apologized. "I woke up late this morning and we missed the show. How about if we go to my house for lunch instead? You can run over and tell Mrs. Newley all about how Goldie is doing."

"Okay," Brandy agreed readily. "Can I bring Goldie? I bet she'd like to see her. Goldie's really grown a lot."

"Sure," Maggie said. She smiled and almost cried. "Let's go get her."

Quickly, she added to herself. She needed to get away from Ryan. Just making it through the day with Brandy without breaking down was going to be difficult enough, she realized, but being in Ryan's presence right now was impossible. She feared she really would fall apart if she didn't get away soon.

The phone across the room rang. Ryan picked up the receiver.

"Maggie?" he asked into the phone, looking up at her with a puzzled expression. "It's for you."

He held the receiver out to her. Maggie walked across the living room and put the phone to her ear. After a quick conversation, she replaced the receiver.

"Wait, Brandy," Maggie said, her heart sinking even further. She stopped the little girl as she opened the back door. Brandy turned and looked at her expectantly. "Something's happened," Maggie explained slowly. She forced herself to check Ryan's expression and met with reserved distance. "There's been a break-in at my office."

Brandy's eyes rounded. "A robbery?" she asked in a hushed voice.

"That's right," Maggie said. She shifted her gaze to Ryan. "Mike wants me to go down there and take inventory for the police. I'll have to analyze the inventory lists and it'll take a long time, Brandy. I'm not going to be able to have lunch with you today. I'm sorry."

"Oh," Brandy said, her expression deflating. "Do you have to go right now? Can you go after lunch?"

"Oh, Brandy, I wish I could. But the police are there now. I have to talk to them. They're waiting for me."

"How did they know to reach you here?" Ryan asked. His countenance revealed an unyielding stiffness.

"My secretary has a list of all the numbers I might be reached at," Maggie explained, a note of defensiveness threading through the words. "They need to be able to contact me. It's part of my job to be available."

She stared at him, hurt mingling with frustration.

"You'd better go," he prodded coolly.

"I'm sorry, Brandy," Maggie said again, leaning down to give Brandy a quick hug. The disappointment in the little girl's face cut her as much as Ryan's dismissive words did.

"It's okay, Maggie," Brandy allowed as she flung her arms around Maggie's waist. "Maybe I can take Goldie to see Mrs. Newley next week."

"Of course you can," Maggie promised, swallowing down another rise of emotion in her throat. As she stood, Ryan's hard eyes met hers briefly and shifted away.

"Goodbye," she told him.

Nodding mutely, Ryan stared again at the spring day through the sliding glass doors. He heard the click of her shoes against the tile in the entry, then the opening and shutting of the oak front door. In his deepest places, he longed to run after her, to stop her.

He slid open the glass door and stepped onto the back patio. The freshness of the May air surrounded him, seeming by contrast to increase the flat dullness in his chest.

From the other side of the house, he heard the sound of Maggie's car as she drove away.

* * *

Maggie slumped onto the couch in her living room, sunset shooting its golden rays between the folds of the opened miniblinds. The hours of answering questions, filling out reports and analyzing missing inventory had effectively pushed her emotions inward to a core of intense hurt. Her head ached from the pressure of it all. She was almost numb from ignoring it.

Letting her head fall back against the cushion, she closed her eyes tiredly.

"How could I let myself fall in love with him?" she whispered in the stillness of her living room.

The phone rang. Maggie considered allowing her machine to pick up, then opened her eyes and leaned forward slowly to lift the receiver to her ear.

"Maggie?" Emma's ever-cheerful voice questioned. "You sound tired. How was your trip? Sounds like it must have worn you out."

"It was okay," Maggie answered tonelessly. "It's not that, really." She told Emma about the burglary.

"What's wrong, Mag?" Emma asked. "I can tell something's wrong. It's not the burglary. It's Ryan, isn't it?"

Maggie sighed, too tired to hedge, and admitted the truth to Emma.

Fifteen minutes later, her friend was beside her on the couch, ready with comfort and advice.

"You did fall in love with him, didn't you? I knew it," Emma said. "You can't give up so easily, Maggie."

"Oh, Emma, it's not that simple," Maggie scoffed, shaking her head. She stopped when the movement provoked a stab of tense pain behind her eyes. "I can't be the person he wants me to be and that's that. He thinks we're too different, that our priorities aren't the same."

"And that's it? The end?" Emma asked in disbelief. She frowned. "You two can't find some ground in between? I don't believe it."

"I don't think there is any ground in between in this situation," Maggie replied, sighing. She rubbed her forehead and around her eyes where the ache was intensifying.

"I hate to see two people who love each other just give up," Emma insisted.

"He doesn't love me," Maggie reminded her in a low voice. "He never said that. He never even said he cared for me."

"Did you tell him you loved him?"

"Of course not, Emma," Maggie answered her, shocked. Emma frowned at her again. "It doesn't matter, anyway," she said. She felt tears behind her eyes. "When he looks at me, he sees his former wife. He's convinced that he and Brandy will always come second to my career."

Emma drew her brows together as she listened.

"Have you shown him that's not true?" she asked.

"I've tried."

Emma shook her head. "He's been burned once, Maggie. You have to keep trying."

Maggie remembered the wounded gleam she'd caught—for just a flickering second—in Ryan's eyes that morning.

"He's afraid, Emma," she whispered.

"He wouldn't be afraid unless he loved you, Maggie." Emma regarded her seriously for several moments. "You have to show him that you're different." She nodded a couple of times in reinforcement of her words.

"I don't know how," Maggie told her softly.

"You'll know," Emma said, shrugging. "Just be you."

Then Emma cooked up a pot of mushroom soup and persisted until Maggie swallowed a few spoonfuls of it with her. Maggie had no appetite, but she had learned a long time ago that when Emma was set on something, it was usually easier to go along with it than to fight it.

Maggie was glad when Emma left, grateful that her friend cared but not feeling up to her lively optimism. She took a couple of aspirins and went to bed early, tired both physically and emotionally from the day. Sinking onto the soft bed, she tried to clear her mind of everything and allow simple exhaustion to swallow her.

Ryan's face loomed up in the darkness as she closed her eyes.

I'm crazy for you, he'd said to her once. He'd never said more than that.

He wouldn't be afraid unless he loved you, Emma had insisted.

Only when she felt the moistness of the sheet against her cheek did Maggie realize she was crying.

Chapter Nine

"Hi, Maggie! Daddy's in the kitchen. I'm not done getting dressed yet." Brandy beamed a broad smile at Maggie, then disappeared down the hall to her bedroom. Maggie stood awkwardly in the entry hall, a large foil-wrapped loaf of fresh, warm bread in one hand. She precariously balanced a single-layer cellophane-covered bunny cake against her chest with the other.

Desperately needing to relieve herself of her burdens, she headed for the kitchen. Ryan, his hands inside heavy yellow mitts, fiddled with the foil cover of a large pan of lasagna in the oven. He looked up at Maggie's approach, standing and pushing shut the oven door with his knee.

Drawing the mitts from his hands, he moved to take the bunny-shaped cake from Maggie. Despite the cool distance that hung between them now, his nearness still inspired the same tingle of awareness in Maggie's veins.

"Hi." She struggled to force a smile as she set the bread on the counter. Brandy's birthday request—dinner with her two favorite grown-ups—promised to be an uncomfortable affair. She'd asked her father to make lasagna, her favorite meal, with Maggie bringing the bread and birthday cake. A small party with Brandy's friends was scheduled for later, following the dinner.

"Thanks for bringing the cake," Ryan said. He lifted the cellophane wrap to inspect the decorating details atop the coconut-covered white icing. "Has Brandy seen it?"

"Not yet," Maggie told him. "She ran off to finish dressing after she answered the door." The mundane course of the conversation unnerved her. How could he act as if nothing had ever happened between them, as if they hadn't begun building something special together, as if he hadn't made her love him?

She realized with a renewed sense of hurt that this was the longest conversation they'd had in the past few weeks. She'd barely seen him since the day of the break-in at her office. Whenever she came to pick up Brandy, Ryan avoided her by always having Brandy ready to go. There had been no delays, no awkward waiting in the living room and having to speak to each other while Brandy got ready.

She'd tried to be angry with him, but had found she couldn't. She'd glimpsed pain in his eyes, too, during the rare moments when they were together. She caught herself hoping he would change his mind, but the finality of their last conversation haunted her. And he seemed to have adjusted to their new, distant relationship with an ease Maggie couldn't yet match.

While his mere closeness never failed to send shivers of longing to her heart, he betrayed no passion, no fire for her that she could see. The sadness in his eyes stemmed simply from regret that he'd hurt her, she told herself. His actions showed plainly that this new "friendship" was how he wanted things to be.

He was quite civilized about it, Maggie thought numbly. He made it seem as if nothing had ever happened.

But something had happened. Maggie had the dullness around her heart to prove it.

She was glad Brandy hadn't seemed to have noticed anything was wrong, glad Ryan had proven true to his word that he wanted her to continue a close relationship with his daughter. And he'd been generous about including her in Brandy's party. But she knew he'd done that for Brandy, not for her.

She watched as Ryan picked up a tomato and a knife and began slicing the ripe, red fruit for the salad. The only sound in the next moment was the steady tap of the knife sliding down against the wooden cutting board.

"Brandy's present is still in the car," Maggie said, and headed out to retrieve it, hoping Brandy would have emerged from her room by the time she returned.

Ryan rested the knife against the cutting board and stared after Maggie. His grip on the knife's handle loosened.

He'd barely had to glance at her to know everything—as if he'd been staring at her all day. Maggie had drawn her auburn curls away from her face with a white ribbon at the nape, revealing the creamy line of her long neck. The contours of her face, delicately drawn and beautiful, suggested the vulnerability lurking just beneath the surface. Her lips, full and soft and touched lightly with pink lipstick, hinted at times past when he could have kissed them.

The thick lushness of her lashes served only to remind him of how she looked when she lowered them in passion, readying for his kiss. Memories of kissing Maggie rushed over Ryan. The knife slid from his fingers as he stared at the empty doorway of the kitchen.

The pungent aroma of oregano and tomato sauce permeated the room, but the soft bewitchment of Maggie's lingering scent filtered through to Ryan. He smiled, immersing himself for a quiet moment in the memory of burying his face in her hair, inhaling the fragrance of her silky red tresses and smooth pale skin.

"Ryan?"

He jumped, startled to realize that Maggie stood in the doorway. She slid a rectangular, wrapped gift atop the refrigerator and gazed at him questioningly.

"Do you need help with anything?" Maggie asked.

"No, thanks," Ryan told her, taking up the knife again and determinedly returning to the salad preparation. "The lasagna is almost ready, and the salad will be done in a few minutes. The table's already set."

Maggie nodded. "Good," she said, then stood there awkwardly, uncertain of what to do next. Quiet reared between them. "Ryan?"

He glanced at her quickly, then returned to his slicing.

"Has—" Maggie hesitated, then pressed ahead. "Has Brandy said anything? I mean, does it seem like she's noticed anything different? Between you and me."

Ryan dumped the chopped tomato from the cutting board into a medium-size bowl and reached for the head of iceberg lettuce draining on a folded paper towel. He tore several large leaves from the lettuce before answering.

"I don't think so," he said finally. "Has she said anything to you?" He glanced briefly, sharply, at Maggie.

"No." Maggie ran her tongue along her lower lip in a nervous gesture. "We haven't spent as much time together in the last few weeks as before when—" She hesitated again. "You'd tell me if she was upset, if she had any nightmares, wouldn't you?"

Ryan set the lettuce down, his gaze locking with Maggie's.

"She hasn't had any nightmares in a long time, Maggie." His eyes were serious. "She's changed since she's been with you. She's more confident. She's happier." He searched Maggie's face a moment before adding, "She's certain that you'll always be there for her."

"She's right." Maggie paused. "Why is it that she can see that and you can't?"

"Oooh, Daddy, my cake!"

Maggie nearly jumped at the sound of Brandy's voice as the little girl rushed past her, eyes wide as she took in the coconut bunny cake. She reached a small finger toward one rich corner.

"No, you don't," Ryan warned his daughter, leaving Maggie's question unanswered, hanging between them. "You have to wait for your party." He shooed Brandy and Maggie toward the dining room. The candlelit room glowed golden, the drapes closed against the sunny early-evening outside.

Maggie sat down in one of the ladder-back chairs, remembering vividly the meal she'd shared with Ryan the night Brandy had taken it upon herself to extend a dinner invitation. The menu that evening had included lasagna, as well, with the same clear, sparkling dishes and tapered white candles that graced the table now in celebration of Brandy's birthday.

That night had been only a couple of months ago, Maggie realized suddenly. It seemed as if years had passed. That night had been the beginning—the first time Ryan had opened up to her, the first time he'd kissed her. She suspected now that she'd begun to fall in love with him that night.

Ryan entered, carrying the tossed salad and sliced bread. Maggie stared up at him, watching the glow of candlelight gleaming in his deep blue eyes. A flicker of knowledge in his darkened depths told her that he remembered that first dinner, too.

He sat down across from her, their hands brushing with electricity when he handed her the bread. She felt his eyes on her throughout the meal, his study provoking a charged awareness that tingled along her skin even when she didn't raise her gaze to meet his.

Brandy chattered, eagerly anticipating the party to follow. When they finished, Ryan washed up while Maggie cleared the table, bringing the dishes in for him as he stood at the sink. Then she cleaned off the table and blew out the tall candles before bringing the cake out to the dining room along with a brightly patterned set of paper plates and napkins for the party.

The children began arriving then, one by one, quickly filling the house with laughter. Gifts piled up on the table, and Maggie brought in her present from the kitchen.

Before long, she and Ryan had gathered the group of giggling girls around the table. Brandy sat in the place of honor before the bunny cake as they all sang a rousing chorus of the traditional birthday song. Her round cheeks glowed pinkly as she leaned forward and blew at the lit birthday candles as hard as she could. Everyone laughed as she had to take a second breath to snuff out a last, recalcitrant candle.

Maggie clapped with the rest, laughing as Brandy shook her head determinedly when several children called out for her to reveal her birthday wish. Ryan's dark head bent to his daughter's and he kissed the top of her head.

"Happy birthday, sweetheart," he said. Brandy smiled up at him, then eagerly turned back to her presents. Picking the first one up, she tore at the wrapping and reached into the box. She pulled out a doll with dark braids like her own. The doll wore a blue dress decorated with lace and ribbons.

"Look, Daddy, this doll looks like me," she cried. Ryan opened the card for her.

"It's from Maggie," he said, looking across the dining room to where Maggie stood behind the crowded table. Maggie met his gaze. In his eyes, she saw his appreciation of the carefully chosen gift. She smiled with satisfaction at Brandy's excitement as the little girl jumped up and scampered around the table to her.

Brandy threw her arms around Maggie and cried, "Thanks, Maggie. I've never had a doll that looked like me before. I love you."

Maggie bent down to return her hug. Over Brandy's shoulder she saw Ryan watching them.

"I love you, too," she told Brandy, awkwardly shifting her eyes from Ryan. "Happy birthday."

Brandy skipped back around to her seat, where she plunged back into her pile of gifts. Maggie followed her.

"Let me cut the cake," she offered to Ryan as he helped Brandy pry open the next box.

"Thank you," he said. Maggie thought she glimpsed a smile of gratitude, but then it was gone.

She noticed throughout the party that he kept looking toward the clock, frowning, and she wondered why. But then he would look back at Brandy and smile, and everything would seem normal again.

Maggie found herself sneaking glances at him as she sliced the frosted bunny cake. It was so hard holding back, stopping herself from touching him when he was so close, only a breath away. But he was determined there would be nothing between them. He'd been clear about that.

Yet she couldn't help remembering the passion that had once flared in his eyes when she was near, the seduction of his hand reaching out to stroke the line of her jaw as he leaned in to kiss her—

Just stop it, she reprimanded herself. She had to stop thinking about him that way.

An hour and a half later, all the presents had been opened, three-fourths of the bunny-shaped cake had been eaten and Brandy was arranging her new toys in her room. The last guest had been picked up by her mother, and Maggie carried the paper plates into the kitchen to the trash.

"You don't have to do that," Ryan said behind her.

"I can't leave you with this mess," Maggie said. "I don't mind."

Ryan opened his mouth to say something, then shut it when the doorbell rang. He turned and headed for the front door. Maggie followed him, deciding it would be best to simply get her purse and go. Now that the party was over, Ryan didn't want her here, and it was too uncomfortable, too painful, to stay any longer.

As the party had progressed, his mood had shifted and she'd begun to suspect that something was bothering him. He'd begun to look irritated, annoyed even. The lingering, intense looks he'd showered her with during dinner had disappeared. No doubt he simply wished she'd leave now that all the other guests had gone.

Maggie picked up her purse and walked down the hall to Brandy's room. She found Brandy sitting on the bed, the doll Maggie had given her held tight in her arms.

"I'm going now, Brandy," Maggie said.

"Thanks for the doll," Brandy said again, and got up to hug Maggie.

"I'm glad you had a wonderful birthday," Maggie told her, kissing her cheek. "See you next weekend."

She turned to go and nearly bumped into Ryan in the doorway. A tall woman with short, blond hair and an artfully made-up face breezed in behind him. She swept past Maggie with an inquisitive glance, then focused on Brandy.

The sophisticated cut of her subdued plum suit and the subtle quality of her tastefully minimal jewelry bespoke success with a capital *S*, Maggie observed quickly.

"Mommy!" Brandy cried.

Maggie froze, her interest immediately arrested.

Brandy bounded over to the woman and flung her arms around her. She hugged her quickly and pulled back. "You missed my party," she accused.

"I know. I'm sorry about that, darling," Delia said. "Look what I brought you."

She held out a bag to her daughter. Brandy opened the bag and pulled out a T-shirt emblazoned with the name of a Georgia sports team.

Maggie thought it looked like the sort of shirt that came from an airport gift shop.

"Thank you, Mommy," Brandy said. She frowned. "But I think it's too small." She held the shirt up to her chest.

"Oh, is it?" Delia laughed and ruffled Brandy's hair playfully. "Well, you're growing like a little weed, aren't you? Don't worry, pumpkin. I'm leaving a check for you with your father. You can buy anything your little heart desires."

Delia sat down on the bed.

Maggie looked at Ryan leaning against the doorjamb. Although his body appeared relaxed, she took in the rigid set of his features and realized this was what he'd been irritated about throughout the party. Although he hid the heat of his expression behind hooded eyes, the tension in his straight lips told Maggie he was angry.

"Like I was telling your dad," Delia said, "the plane was delayed getting out of Atlanta. I'd arranged to have a stopover here on my way to Washington. I was going to have a good two hours to spend with you so I could be at your party, but since my first plane got off late, I'll have to go right back to the airport. I'm spending the week in Washington, D.C. on business for my firm." She glanced down at her slim gold watch. "I have about half an hour. Tell me all about school, honey."

Maggie murmured something about having to go, uneasy with being present during Brandy's mother's visit. She felt Delia eyeing her curiously as she moved to leave.

"Mommy, you didn't meet Maggie," Brandy said.

Maggie smiled stiffly and introduced herself as a friend of Brandy's, hoping to get out with just that. Brandy piped in after her, however, explaining all about the community center program.

"Maggie's taken me to all kinds of neat places," Brandy said, reeling off a list of their recent excursions. "And she teaches me things, too. She taught me to make bread, didn't she, Daddy?"

Ryan nodded. Delia's lips formed a smile, but it failed to reach her eyes.

"Isn't that nice," she said. "Bread. I don't have time for that sort of thing myself, but I've heard it can be quite a therapeutic activity. Of course, I hope Brandy won't get too caught up in these domestic pursuits. There's so much else to life, right, pumpkin?"

Dismissing Maggie, she turned back to Brandy and began describing her trip to Washington.

Maggie slipped out of Brandy's room with a quiet goodbye to Ryan as she passed him. She didn't realize until she reached the front door that he'd followed her down the hallway.

"Thanks for everything," he said.

"No problem," Maggie shrugged. She felt suddenly nervous, tongue-tied, and in that moment he looked as if he felt the same.

She said goodbye again and he held the door open for her as she stepped out onto the stone path to the street. She felt his eyes burning into her back as she reached her car and got in. She could see him through her rearview mirror, still standing in the doorway, watching as she drove away.

Ryan shut the door as the glow of Maggie's taillights disappeared into the darkness. He sat down on the couch in the living room, waiting for Delia.

She came in and stood in the opening between the entry and the living room. He watched her, saying nothing. She gave up waiting for an invitation and came in and sat down in the chair across from him.

"Brandy's getting ready for bed," she said. "I've already told her goodbye."

Ryan nodded.

"I want to know who this woman is."

"Her name's Maggie Wells."

"What's she doing with Brandy?" Delia eyed him narrowly. "Why does Brandy need to be in this sort of program?"

Ryan tilted his head and assessed his former wife coolly. "Your daughter needs this sort of program because she doesn't have a mother," Ryan said, his voice calm and emotionless.

"That's ridiculous." Delia pursed her lips, waiting. When Ryan made no response, she sighed. "Well, here's the check." She handed Ryan a folded paper. "Sorry I didn't get a chance to shop for her."

She stood and moved toward the door. Ryan followed, holding the front door open for her.

"Delia?"

She turned in the doorway and stared back at him.

"Why haven't you remarried?" he asked her, the words blurted out faster than he could stop them. He froze then, waiting for her to answer.

Delia drew her brows together curiously.

"I tried marriage once, remember? You were there." She stared at him seriously. "I might try again someday. But not for a long time. I'm just—" She hesitated. Her perfect poise lapsed briefly and she looked uncertain. "I'm just not ready." She shook her head. "But what about you, Ryan?" Her expression softened slightly. "You were always the family type."

Ryan stared at her, and after a moment she glanced at her watch. Then, without waiting for an answer to her question, she said goodbye and turned away to head down the flagged walk. With a brief wave, she slid into her airport rental car and drove away.

Ryan glanced up at Brandy as he finished the second chapter from a new book he'd given her earlier as one of her birthday gifts. Her bright eyes told him quickly that she was still keyed-up from the busy day.

Resolutely he closed the book and reached for her lamp switch.

"It's time for you to go to sleep," he told her, clicking off the lamp. He leaned down to kiss her. "Happy birthday, sweetheart," he told her again.

"Mommy didn't even try to come to my party," Brandy said suddenly. Ryan narrowed his gaze at her, noting the serious glow in her round eyes in the dim light that filtered in from the hall.

"She wanted to be here," Ryan assured her. "Her plane was delayed."

"Maggie was here," Brandy said. "Maggie always comes when I really need her. She would never miss anything like a birthday party."

Ryan hugged his daughter close, a tight pain closing in on his throat. He knew, suddenly and sharply, that his daughter was right. Maggie would have moved heaven and earth to be at Brandy's birthday party. She might miss a lunch date, or a theater show, but never a birthday.

A familiar yearning burned through him as he thought of Maggie with her creamy skin, vulnerable, sweet eyes and giving heart. She'd given and given and given—to Brandy and to him. And had never asked for anything in return.

"Daddy? Can I tell you what I wished for when I blew out my birthday candles?"

"If you want to," Ryan told Brandy, still seeing Maggie in his mind's eye.

"I wished you'd marry Maggie."

Chapter Ten

"Maggie?"

Turning to the little girl sitting beside her on the park bench, Maggie smiled softly as she waited for her to continue. The expression on Brandy's face touched her with its serious intensity.

"Do you want to know what I wished for at my party?" Brandy asked finally. She chewed on her bottom lip as she stared up at Maggie.

"Wishes don't come true if you tell them," Maggie warned her.

She placed her arm around Brandy's shoulders and hugged her. They were quiet a moment, sitting in the shade to escape the late afternoon's June heat. Goldie romped playfully in the thick grass surrounding them. For their first outing since Brandy's birthday party, Maggie had brought Brandy and her rambunctious puppy to the park to run and play for a few hours.

"Keeping wishes secret doesn't make them come true," Brandy said. "I wished lots of times that my mom and dad would get married again, but it never happened. Besides," she added, grinning impishly, "I already told Daddy about my wish."

"Well, then you've already stretched your luck," she advised Brandy, smiling.

The little girl shook her head emphatically. "I want to tell you about it," she insisted. "Maybe if I tell you what I wished, you can make it come true."

"Oh, I don't know if I can do that," Maggie answered her. "But I guess it would be okay if you really want to tell me your wish."

"I wished that my dad would marry you," Brandy told her, a proud lilt to her voice.

Maggie's breath caught in her throat as the little girl spoke. Her heart pumped faster.

She'd told Ryan this wish?

"Brandy, what would make you wish that?"

Brandy looked up at her somberly.

"Well, you're fun," she replied. "And you're nice. You take me to do neat things. I think you'd be a neat mom."

"Oh, Brandy, thank you." Maggie squeezed her shoulders. "But I don't have to marry your dad to do fun things with you. We're friends, remember?"

"Always?"

"Yes, always," Maggie repeated.

"Well, I still think it'd be neat if you married my dad," Brandy persisted.

"I'll take that as a compliment." She hesitated. "What did your father say when you told him your wish?"

Brandy made a face. "He told me to go to sleep," she said.

Maggie felt as if her heart had dropped to her stomach. *What did you expect?* she berated herself. Ryan had told her in no uncertain terms that he didn't believe a romantic relationship between the two of them would work.

But the night of Brandy's birthday party, in spite of everything, Maggie had allowed herself moments to dream that he might change his mind. The intensity of his gaze during the candlelit dinner, the way he'd watched her as she drove away—his expression had seemed almost wistful when she looked back on the evening.

She sighed, forcing the thoughts away. The whole idea of Ryan changing his mind about her was ridiculous, she told herself. After all, a week had passed since Brandy's birthday party. Ryan's behavior had been perfectly ordinary when she'd picked Brandy up for their park outing. The wistful look no doubt stemmed from her own wishful thinking.

"Time to go," Maggie announced, bringing her arm out from around Brandy's shoulders as she took her hand to pull her up. "I need to get ready for the awards banquet I told you about earlier, remember? And your father is expecting you for supper. Come on." She glanced around for Goldie, realizing suddenly that the dog was no longer playing by their bench.

"Goldie?" Brandy called, looking about her with a suddenly frantic air. "Goldie! Where is she, Maggie?"

"I don't know. Do you think she's gone back over to the playground?"

"I didn't see her go over there." Brandy's voice cracked. "She was right here. What happened to her?"

"Come on. Let's go look on the playground, just in case," Maggie said calmly. "Don't worry. We'll find her."

Brandy flew across the park, dark braids bopping against her back. She called for the dog in a high, frightened voice. Maggie followed at a quick pace.

Brandy ran from the swings to the slide, then to Maggie.

"She's not here! I've lost her." Her face crumpled.

Maggie bent down to comfort her.

"We'll look all over the park, Brandy," she promised. "We'll look everywhere. She's bound to be here somewhere."

She took Brandy's hand and set off confidently, pushing back the thought that she needed to hurry. As it was, she'd stayed at the park until the last minute, cutting rather close her time to prepare for the banquet.

As they walked, she glimpsed Goldie out of the corner of her eye. The dog streaked past them, chasing a small white cat toward the opposite side of the park and into the street.

"There she is!" Brandy screamed.

Brandy tugged her hand from Maggie and raced after the dog. Maggie ran after her; then they both stopped, frozen, as a small red car turned the corner and thudded into Goldie.

The car screeched to a halt and the driver jumped out, leaving his door hanging open as he ran around the car to the fallen dog. The cat disappeared through a tall hedge on the other side of the road.

Maggie roused herself from the shock of the instant and ran to Brandy.

"They hit Goldie," Brandy said in a tiny voice. Tears flooded her cheeks.

"Wait here," Maggie instructed Brandy, but didn't try to stop the little girl when she followed her to the road.

Maggie knelt down beside the driver of the car to lean over the injured dog. Fright radiated from Goldie's brown eyes, and her chest heaved. Brandy fell to the pavement beside Maggie a moment later, a small cry escaping her lips as she stared down at her wounded puppy.

"She's still breathing," the driver said shakily. "Is this your dog? I'm so sorry. I didn't see her."

"Maggie, help her!" Brandy wailed. Maggie comforted the little girl with a gentle hug, carefully hiding her concern as they hovered over the injured dog. Goldie was breathing, it was true, but Maggie saw the pain and terror in the dog's velvety brown eyes.

She had no idea how badly the dog might be hurt.

"Stay here," Maggie told her firmly. This time Brandy obeyed her as Maggie ran back across the park and drove her car around. The driver that had hit Goldie helped Maggie gingerly lift the dog to the front seat of the sports car, jarring the pet as little as possible. Brandy climbed into the back.

"Don't worry, Brandy," Maggie soothed as she headed directly for Romeo's veterinarian. Glancing at the clock in her dash, she noted the time. Romeo's vet kept late Saturday hours. "We're going to get help for her."

Brandy leaned forward as far as her seat belt would allow and watched Goldie with worried eyes.

"Be okay, Goldie," she whispered, her voice breaking. "Please be okay."

Ryan pushed open the glass door of the veterinarian's office. His gaze was drawn immediately to Maggie, her auburn curls floating around her shoulders, concern gleaming in the green eyes that rose to meet his. Brandy sat huddled in the crook of Maggie's shoulder, her face wet with tears.

"Daddy!" she cried when she saw him and ran to him, flinging her arms around him. Ryan bent down to hug her tightly, questioning Maggie with his eyes.

Maggie shook her head.

"They don't know anything yet," she told him. She glanced down at her watch. "We got here about half an hour ago. It was a few minutes before I could call you." Brandy climbed up on the seat beside her and leaned into her shoulder again. Ryan sat down beside his daughter. "Brandy's been terribly upset." Maggie stroked the top of Brandy's head, looking over her to Ryan. "She saw it happen."

She saw her own worry mirrored in Ryan's eyes.

"Is Goldie going to die?" Brandy asked, tilting her head up to her father.

Maggie watched Ryan's expression, tender and concerned, as he looked at his daughter. He kissed her on the forehead.

"I'm sure they're doing their best to make Goldie better, sweetheart," he told her. "We have to wait for the doctor to tell us how Goldie's doing." He glanced back to Maggie. "Did they say how long it would be before they'd let us know anything?"

Maggie shrugged. "She was in shock when we brought her in here. They said they would give her some medication for that, and they're going to X-ray her to check for broken bones." Her gaze fell to her watch. She should have been home thirty minutes ago—dressing in the burgundy suit she'd bought exclusively for the awards banquet, applying her makeup, fixing her hair. And driving downtown to the hotel where the banquet was being held.

Ryan noticed the quiet way Maggie stared down at her watch, the serious set to her lips as she noted the time. An unexpected streak of jealousy surged through him as he wondered if she had plans for the evening—plans that included a male companion.

You have no right to care about her personal life, he told himself. But the warning had no effect. He wanted to have the right to care.

He'd spent every night since Brandy's birthday party thinking about Maggie. He'd almost picked up the phone to call her a dozen times.

But still he'd held back, that old, stubborn fear wrapped around him like a safety net.

Now, seeing her staring surreptitiously at her watch, he suddenly feared he'd waited too long.

"Maggie?" He watched her soft, green eyes rise to his. "If you have someplace you need to be—"

"No! Don't go, Maggie," Brandy cried, turning to throw her arms tightly around Maggie's waist.

"Brandy—" Ryan began.

"Please stay," Brandy begged.

The little girl's blue eyes, darkened with hurt, stabbed into Maggie's heart. She brushed back the wisps of hair coming loose from Brandy's braids, then hugged her.

"I'm not going anywhere," she told Brandy. "I promise. Not until we know how Goldie is."

Ryan watched as Maggie held Brandy, rocking her gently in her embrace. Longing to be a part of their warm circle, he shifted closer, snaking his arm around Brandy until he just barely touched Maggie's shoulder. Her lashes flashed up, surprise in the quick glitter of light in her eyes. Then she moved, almost imperceptibly, toward him, and together they formed a soothing cocoon for Brandy.

Ryan began talking in a low voice about Goldie and the tricks she'd learned. Maggie soon caught on to his attempt to distract Brandy, and related a few stories of her own of times Goldie had jumped on her or surprised her with her playfulness. Brandy quickly joined in until all three of them were softly laughing at the recollections of the puppy's antics.

Maggie determinedly avoided her watch. She knew without looking that she was dreadfully late for the banquet.

She imagined Mike Roberts looking for her, her name being called when they announced the list of nominees. Then she glanced at Brandy's face, washed of much of her earlier distress. And she looked into Ryan's eyes, relaxed and kind as they rested on her.

She was glad she'd stayed. Warmth rushed over her from the intense power of Ryan's gaze.

His expression was almost *loving,* she thought. Then she wondered where such an outrageous idea had come from. Ryan merely felt gratitude, she reminded herself.

"Goldie's doing pretty good right now," the veterinarian said as he entered the waiting area, breaking abruptly into Maggie's reverie. She stared up at him, then down at Brandy, who gazed solemnly at the doctor. "We've given her some pain medication and she's resting now. The X rays revealed she does have a broken left hind leg, but we'll have to wait a couple of days before we can set it."

"Wait?" Ryan's face showed surprise.

"We have to be certain there aren't also internal injuries," the veterinarian explained. "We can't place her under an anesthetic to set the bone until we know the full extent of her injuries. It'll take a couple of days for the swelling to go down enough for us to make a determination."

"And if there are internal injuries?" Ryan asked.

The veterinarian's face took on a grave cast. His eyes shifted to Brandy, then back to Ryan.

"Things look good as they are," he said slowly. "A broken leg will heal. Internal injuries make for a touchier recovery. We'll know more about her condition by morning. If she's eating and drinking tomorrow, it'll be a good sign that there aren't any other injuries. For now, we'll have to wait and see. She's resting comfortably. There's nothing for you to do now but go home and call in the morning."

The doctor disappeared back through the swinging doors that led to the rear examining rooms. Brandy continued to sit very still, as she had throughout the doctor's talk.

"Is Goldie going to be okay?" she asked in a small voice.

Ryan hugged her. "I hope so," he said softly. He rose, pulling Brandy up with him. "We just have to wait, sweetie. We'll call in the morning and see how she is, okay?"

Brandy chewed on her lower lip, worry still etched on her small features, but nodded obediently as she stood beside her father. She slipped her hand into his as she leaned against him.

Maggie reached for her purse and car keys, then knelt to offer Brandy a last encouraging kiss on the cheek. A glance at her watch told her she might just have time to walk into the banquet hall in time to hear the award announced. If she hurried.

"Thanks for staying with me, Maggie," Brandy said softly.

Maggie smiled at her. "Anytime. We're friends, remember?" She kissed her again. When she stood up, she felt Ryan's gaze on her and turned to meet his eyes. He met hers with a serious expression.

"Thank you," he said.

She had a strange feeling that he'd almost said something else, then changed his mind. Uncomfortable under his scrutiny, she murmured a quick goodbye.

Ryan watched Maggie walk to her car as he stood at the counter, waiting for the receptionist to prepare his payment information. There was no doubt about it. Maggie had plans for the evening. And she'd held them up while she stayed to attend Brandy.

"Daddy?"

He looked down at Brandy.

"Maggie's going to be late for her awards banquet, isn't she?" Brandy stared at him.

"Awards banquet?" Ryan repeated, stunned. He glanced back out at the parking lot. Maggie's car had disappeared.

Maggie woke slowly, not realizing at first that the sound waking her was the doorbell. She leaned up sleepily, reaching for the robe that lay on the chair by her bed. She padded clumsily to the door, still more asleep than awake. She peered fuzzily into the peep-hole.

Clear blue eyes set in an angular face topped by chestnut waves met her gaze.

Ryan?

She stepped back, blinked and looked again. Then she looked down at her faded blue terry-cloth robe in dismay. She ran back to her closet. She shrugged off the blue robe, allowing it to fall carelessly to the closet floor. Leaving on the short, lace-edged satiny gown she wore beneath, she slipped into a matching white robe and ran back to the door, refusing to analyze why she did it.

She glimpsed herself in passing in her dresser mirror. Her pale face, framed by disorderly auburn curls, stared back with anxious green eyes. The thought came to her that she looked a bit like a deer caught in headlights.

Ryan was pounding on her front door by the time she reached the living room again. Maggie opened the door a crack.

"Ryan!" She said his name as if surprised it was him at the door. "I'm really not up."

"Please let me in."

Maggie ran one shaking hand over her hair and pulled the robe tight about her. She edged open the door shyly as Romeo curled about her ankles, mewing for his breakfast.

Ryan pushed the door wide and strode through, taking in her disheveled appearance with interest. His eyes traveled from her face to the formfitting robe. The white wrap ended just above her knees, revealing long, well-shaped calves and slim ankles. Her feet were bare.

"I told you, I'm not up," Maggie said, an awkward note of defensiveness creeping into her voice. The sapphire eyes that rose to her face shot waves of heat through her veins.

She almost wished she'd left the terry robe on. Almost.

Shutting the door, she moved into the kitchen. She felt him follow her by the tingle of awareness in her body that his presence always created.

"I can see that you haven't been up long," he continued.

Maggie turned at his voice, noticing the soft smile lurking gently about his lips as his study raked over her robed form again. His eyes turned back up to her face and his expression settled into more serious lines.

"I'm sorry about yesterday afternoon, if that's why you're here," Maggie told him nervously. She turned her back to him as she started making coffee, determined to do something—anything—with her hands.

And she had to have someplace else to look but into Ryan's probing gaze.

She poured water from the glass carafe into the coffeemaker, then turned on the appliance. The crackle and whoosh of water beginning to percolate through the machine filled the quiet of the kitchen.

Finally, with nothing left to do, she turned and bumped into Ryan, close behind her. The musky maleness of his scent surrounded her. The brush of his arm against hers shot ripples of electricity from her head to her toes.

She stepped away, busying herself by reaching for coffee cups in a cabinet. Setting two mugs in front of the coffeemaker, she looked around desperately for something else to do and found nothing. She stared at Ryan, swallowing uncomfortably.

"I feel responsible," she blurted out. Ryan frowned, and she continued in a rush, "I should have kept better tabs on Goldie at the park." She hesitated, completely uncertain of why Ryan would come to her house at such an early hour. "And maybe I should have waited until you got there before I authorized a lot of expensive treatment for Goldie. I'll pay if you want me to. It just seemed important that they begin treating her right away."

She was babbling, and she couldn't stop herself. The way he was staring at her had her nerves completely shattered.

"I don't want you to pay," Ryan said, shaking his head. "I would have done the same thing myself. I'm grateful you did it." He stepped closer. Maggie started to move away another step before realizing he'd cornered her in the rear of the kitchen.

"I wish Brandy hadn't seen the accident," Maggie told him, leaning against the wall. "She seemed so upset. She didn't have nightmares, did she?"

Ryan noticed the uncertain flicker of her eyes as she watched him, the nervous way she brushed back the tumble of fiery curls behind her shoulders. The vulnerability of the gesture touched his heart and made hope surge in his veins.

"No, she didn't have any nightmares," Ryan said. In answer to the question in Maggie's eyes, he added, "She's at our neighbor's house for the morning." He reached out to Maggie, bridging the short space between them by taking her hand into his.

A sizzling sensation shot through Maggie's arm to the rest of her body. She felt her eyes pulled into his, swallowed in their depths. The intense longing that he always kindled in her soul flamed to the surface.

"Is Goldie okay?" Maggie asked shakily, afraid of where the conversation was leading. Afraid he was suddenly going to pull back from her again, and knowing she couldn't bear to open her soul to him again and lose him. "Have you talked to the vet this morning?"

She tried to remove her hand from his, but he wouldn't release her. Instead, he drew her toward him until his chest brushed hers. Their bodies were so close, she realized, that if he only moved his other arm to her shoulder, they would be in an embrace. Remembered passion shivered up her spine.

"Goldie's going to be fine," Ryan said, so near she felt his breath warm on her cheek. "I called the vet this morning and he told me she was eating and drinking. He doubts she sustained any internal injuries. But that's not why I'm here. This has nothing to do with Goldie. Or Brandy.''

Then why are you here? Maggie wanted to demand. But the question terrified her.

The kitchen was suddenly very quiet. Golden morning light beamed in from the window over the sink, shooting glittering highlights through Ryan's chestnut waves. His blue eyes burned into hers, steady and serious.

''I think the coffee's ready,'' she whispered, glancing toward the coffeemaker on the counter. She tried to focus on the rich, dark liquid steaming in the carafe, but all she could do was inhale the potent masculinity of Ryan's scent and feel the tingle of desire that passed between their barely touching bodies.

''I didn't come here for coffee,'' Ryan said huskily. He pulled Maggie by the hand, bringing her even closer until he felt the softness of her breasts pressed against his chest. With his other hand, he lifted her chin upward, guiding her until she had to stare directly into his eyes. ''I told you once that you amaze me. Do you remember that?''

Maggie nodded, captured by the earnestness of his voice and the honesty of his eyes.

''It meant a lot to Brandy that you took Goldie to the vet and stayed there with her while we waited,'' he continued softly. ''Especially since it meant you were missing your awards banquet.'' Maggie's eyes flickered, but Ryan spoke again quickly. ''She told me after you left that you were going to be late for your banquet. You never said anything to me about it while we were waiting. I know how important this award was to you. Why didn't you tell me?''

"I don't know," Maggie said, the words coming out low and uncertain. "Brandy was upset. She needed me. It just didn't seem important." She hesitated, running her tongue over her suddenly dry lips. "I guess I wasn't sure you would care."

With his other hand Ryan reached up and touched Maggie's face, one finger feathering a trail of sparks along her cheek.

"Maggie." He said her name in a tender voice that was hardly audible, yet felt like an emotional caress to Maggie's ears. "I care." He leaned forward slightly to kiss her earlobe, then her neck. "I can't stop caring.

"I tried to tell myself I didn't care," he continued, his breath close against her cheek. He moved his head to face her, drawing her into the depths of his azure eyes. "But the truth is that I love you, Maggie Wells."

Ryan smiled, his heart free and full as he watched her reaction to his words, words that sometime in the middle of the night he'd come to realize were true. Maggie's lips parted slightly, her emerald eyes darkening as she listened. Reaching up, he tangled his fingers into the satin thickness of her hair, reveling in the feel of her auburn curls in his hands. He yearned to kiss her again, to pull her into his arms and show her the depth of his emotion, but he held back, needing her response.

"Ryan," Maggie began, her thoughts whirling, wanting to seize his words and never let go, yet afraid. "I can't change to be who you want. My career is an important part of my life and that's not going to change. I love you, too," she admitted, searching his eyes. "But I don't want to pretend that I'll be anything different than what I am."

"I don't want you to change," Ryan told her, moving his hands to her shoulders and facing her seriously. "I've been seeing you through my memories of Delia, and that was wrong. You're not anything like her. You've hit me in the face so many times with that truth, and I've been too stubborn—too afraid—to see it. You've proven over and over that you have room in your life and your heart for more than your career." A trickle of fear fingered through his chest. "I hope I haven't realized it too late."

"No, it's not too late," Maggie whispered.

"Did Brandy tell you her birthday wish?"

Maggie's heart nearly stopped beating. "Yes."

"Will you marry me?"

"Oh, Ryan—" And then his mouth covered hers and she met him eagerly as he drew her against him.

He released her at last, breathless and happy.

"I almost let my past destroy my future," he said, unable to resist touching her as he spoke. He ran his fingers along the line of her jaw, delighting in the silky feel of her smooth skin beneath his hand, almost awed by the reality of holding her again. "I think I've been in love with you from the moment I met you at the community center." He smiled as he noted the pink color that rose to Maggie's cheeks. "I've been so afraid of losing you—"

"I'm not going anywhere." Maggie pressed her finger to his lips, stopping his words, then slowly moved her touch down to his chest.

Ryan wrapped his arms tightly around her, snuggling her into his chest. She leaned her head against the cool cotton of his shirt and smiled. "I love you—you and Brandy both."

"I know," he whispered, hugging her. Silence settled over them, then Ryan suddenly pulled back and stared at her. "What about the awards banquet? Did you win?"

Maggie laughed.

"Oh, I made it to the banquet," she told him. "So I was a little late. Okay, maybe a lot late." She shrugged. "But I did arrive before they announced the award. I didn't win." She cast a flirtatious grin at Ryan, easing the concern that flashed into his eyes. "But there's always next year. I never give up, you know."

"I think I've noticed that quality about you," he said. He moved his hand down her back in an enticing stroke. He could feel a thin gown beneath the white robe. "I wonder what Mrs. Fletcher will say when we invite her to our wedding," he murmured, slipping his fingers around to her front and sliding them along the front edge of the wrap where it came together above her breasts.

The gleam in Maggie's green eyes held love and promise and forever. He moved his hand down to finger the sash suggestively.

"I think she'll say you're too old to get matched up in the women's outreach program," Maggie teased him, a ribbon of desire wrapping around her as she felt his hands at her waist.

"That's okay," Ryan returned, his voice taking on a husky note. "I think it's time we start our own program—just as soon as I make you Mrs. Conner."

He bent his head to Maggie again, drawing her close. As their lips joined, she shared her warmth with him in the loving fulfillment of his embrace.

* * * * *

MILLION DOLLAR SWEEPSTAKES

No purchase necessary. To enter, follow the directions published. For eligibility, entries must be received no later than March 31, 1998. No liability is assumed for printing errors, lost, late, nondelivered or misdirected entries. Odds of winning are determined by the number of eligible entries distributed and received.

Sweepstakes open to residents of the U.S. (except Puerto Rico), Canada and Europe who are 18 years of age or older. All applicable laws and regulations apply. Sweepstakes offer void wherever prohibited by law. This sweepstakes is presented by Torstar Corp., its subsidiaries and affiliates, in conjunction with book, merchandise and/or product offerings. For a copy of the Official Rules (WA residents need not affix return postage), send a self-addressed, stamped envelope to: Million Dollar Sweepstakes Rules, P.O. Box 4469, Blair, NE 68009-4469.

SWP-M96